IRÈNE NÉMIROVSKY

The Courilof Affair

TRANSLATED FROM THE FRENCH BY
Sandra Smith

VINTAGE BOOKS
London

Published by Vintage 2008

2 4 6 8 10 9 7 5 3 1

First published in Great Britain in 2007 by Chatto & Windus

Vintage
Random House, 20 Vauxhall Bridge Road,
London SW1V 2SA

www.vintage-books.co.uk

Addresses for companies within The Random House Group Limited
can be found at: www.randomhouse.co.uk/offices.htm

The Random House Group Limited Reg. No. 954009

A CIP catalogue record for this book
is available from the British Library

ISBN 9780099493983

The Random House Group Limited supports the Forest
Stewardship Council (FSC), the leading international forest
certification organisation. All our titles that are printed on
Greenpeace approved FSC certified paper carry the FSC logo.
Our paper procurement policy can be found at
www.rbooks.co.uk/environment

Typeset by Palimpsest Book Production Limited,
Grangemouth, Stirlingshire

Printed in the UK by CPI Bookmarque, Croydon, CR0 4TD

THE COURILOF AFFAIR

Irène Némirovsky was born in Kiev in 1903, the daughter of a successful Jewish banker. In 1918 her family fled the Russian Revolution for France where she became a bestselling novelist, author of *David Golder*, *Le Bal* and other works published in her lifetime, as well as the posthumous *Suite Française*. Prevented from publishing when the Germans occupied France in 1940, she stayed with her husband and two small daughters in the small village of Issy-l'Evêque (in German occupied territory) where she had moved from Paris just before the invasion. In July 1942 she was arrested and interned in Pithiviers concentration camp, and from there immediately deported to Auschwitz where she died in August 1942.

Prologue

Two men sat down separately at the empty tables on the terrace of a café in Nice, attracted by the red flames of a small brazier.

It was autumn, at dusk, on a day that felt cold for that part of the world. 'It's like the sky in Paris . . .' said a woman passing by, pointing to the yellowish clouds carried along by the wind. Within a few moments, it began to rain, enhancing the darkness of the deserted street where the lamps had not yet been lit; raindrops dripped down here and there through the soaked canvas awning stretched over the café.

The man who had followed Léon M on to the terrace had secretly watched him ever since he'd sat down, trying to remember who he was; both men leaned forward towards the warm stove at the same moment.

From inside the café came the muddled sound of voices, people calling out; the crashing of billiard balls, trays banging down on the wooden tables, chess pieces being moved around the boards. Now and again, you could make out the hesitant, shrill fanfare of a small band, muffled by the other noise in the café.

Léon M looked up, pulled his grey wool scarf more tightly around his neck; the man sitting opposite him said quietly: 'Marcel Legrand?'

At the very same moment, the electric lights suddenly came on in the street, in the doorways, and outside the cafés. Surprised by the sudden brightness, Léon M looked away for a moment.

'Marcel Legrand?' the man repeated.

There was a surge of electricity in the street-lights, no doubt, for they grew dimmer; the light flickered for a second, like the flame of a candle left outdoors; then it seemed to come back again, bathing Léon M's face, hunched shoulders, gaunt hands, and delicate wrists in a dazzling light.

'Weren't you in charge of the Courilof affair, in 1903?'

'In 1903?' M repeated slowly.

He tilted his head to the side and whistled softly, with the weary, sarcastic look of a cautious old bird.

The man sitting opposite him was sixty-five; his face looked grey and tired; his upper lip twitched with a nervous tic, causing his big white moustache, once blond, to jump now and again, revealing his pale mouth, his bitter, anxious frown. His lively eyes, piercing and suspicious, quickly lit up and then almost immediately looked away.

'Sorry. I don't recognise you,' M finally said, shrugging his shoulders. 'My memory isn't very good these days . . .'

'Do you remember the detective who used to be Courilof's body guard? The one who ran after you one night, in the Caucasus? . . .'

'The one who ran after me . . . unsuccessfully? I remember now,' said M.

He gently rubbed his hands together; they were getting numb. He was about fifty years old, but he looked older and ill. He had a narrow chest, a dark, sarcastic expression, a beautiful but odd mouth, bad, broken teeth, greying locks of hair spilling over his forehead. His eyes, deeply set, shone with a dim flame.

'Cigarette?' he murmured.

'Do you live in Nice, Monsieur Legrand?'

'Yes.'

'Withdrawn from active service, if I may put it that way?'

'You may.'

M took a puff of his cigarette, without inhaling, watched it burn in his fingers, and threw it down on the ground, slowly stubbing it out with his heel.

'That all happened a long time ago,' he finally said, with a wry smile, 'a very long time ago . . .'

'Yes . . . I was the one responsible for the inquiry, after your arrest, after the terrorist attack.'

'Oh, were you?' M murmured indifferently.

'I never managed to find out your real name. Not one of our secret agents knew who you were, either in Russia or abroad. Now that it doesn't matter any more, tell me something – you were one of the leaders of that terrorist group in Switzerland, before 1905, weren't you?'

'I was never one of the leaders of a terrorist group, just a subordinate.'

'So?'

M nodded, a weary little smile on his face.

'That's how it was, Monsieur.'

'Really, and what about later on? In 1917 and after? I know I'm right, you were really . . .'

He paused, looking for the appropriate word; then he smiled, revealing long, sharp teeth gleaming between pale lips. 'You were really in the thick of it," he said, tracing the shape of a big cauldron in the air. "I mean . . . at the top.'

'Yes . . . at the top.'

'The secret police? The Tcheka?'

'Well, my friend, I did a bit of everything. During those difficult times, everyone lent a hand.'

He tapped out a tune on the marble table with his delicate, curved fingers.

'Won't you tell me your name?' the man said, laughing. 'I swear I'm also peacefully retired now, like you. I ask out of simple curiosity, professional inquisitiveness, if you will.'

M slowly raised the collar of his raincoat and pulled his scarf tighter with the same cautious gesture he always used.

'I don't believe you,' he said, laughing slightly and coughing at the same time. 'People are always drawn back to their first love. And, besides, my name wouldn't tell you anything more now. Everyone forgot it a long time ago.'

'Are you married?'

'No, I've kept some of the good old revolutionary traditions,' said M, smiling again; he had a little mechanical smile that made deep ridges at the corner of his mouth. He picked up a piece of bread and ate it slowly. 'What about you?' he asked, raising his eyebrows. 'What's your name, Monsieur?'

'Oh, my name? No mystery there . . . Baranof . . . Ivan

Ivanitch . . . I was assigned to His Excellency, to Courilof, for ten years.'

'Oh, really?'

For the first time, M's weary little smile faded; up until now, he'd been staring across at the harshly lit wax mannequins, the only items on display in the rain-drenched street, but he stopped staring, coughed slightly, looked straight at Baranof: 'What about his family? Do you know what happened to them?'

'His wife was shot during the Revolution. The children must still be alive. Poor Courilof. We used to call him the Killer Whale. Do you remember?'

'Ferocious and voracious,' said M.

He crumpled the remainder of his bread, started to get up, but it was still pouring; the rain bounced heavily off the pavement in bright sparks. He slowly sat down again.

'Well, you got him,' said Baranof. 'How many others did you personally bag, in total?'

'Then? Or afterwards?'

'In total,' Baranof repeated.

M shrugged his shoulders. 'You know, you remind me of a young man who came to interview me once, in Russia, for an American magazine. He was very interested in the statistics, wanted to know how many men I'd killed since I'd come to power. When I hesitated, he innocently asked: "Is it possible? Is it possible that you can't remember?" He was a rosy-cheeked little Jew by the name of Blumenthal, from the *Chicago Tribune*.'

He motioned to the doorman who was walking between the tables outside: 'Get me that cab.'

The cab stopped in front of the café.

5

He stood up, extended his hand to Baranof.

'It's funny running into each other like this . . .'

'Terribly funny.'

M laughed suddenly. 'And . . . actually . . .' he said in Russian, 'how many people did die? "In answer to our prayers"? With our help?'

'Huh!' said Baranof, shrugging his shoulders. 'Well I, at least, was acting under orders. I don't give a damn.'

'Fair enough,' said M, his voice weary and indifferent. He carefully opened his large black umbrella and lit a cigarette on the brazier. The bright flame suddenly illuminated his face with its hollow cheeks that were the colour of earth, and his wide, suspicious dark eyes. As usual, he didn't actually smoke his cigarette, just breathed in its aroma for a moment, half closed his eyes, then threw it away. He gestured good-bye and left.

Léon M died in March 1932, in the house in Nice where he had spent his final years.

Amongst his books was found a small black leather briefcase; it contained several dozen typed pages clipped together. The first page had written on it, in pencil, the words:

THE COURILOF AFFAIR

1

In 1903, the Revolutionary Committee gave me the responsibility of *liquidating* Courilof. That was the term they
used at the time. This affair was linked to the rest of my
life only in a minor sort of way, but as I am about to
write my autobiography, it stands out in my memory. It
forms the beginnings of my life as a revolutionary, even
though I changed sides afterwards.

Fourteen years passed before I came to power, half of
them spent in prison, half in exile. Then came the October
Revolution (*Sturm und Drang Period*) and another exile.

I have been alive for fifty years, years that have gone
quickly by, and I don't have much to complain about. But
still the final years seem long . . . the end is dragging on.

I was born in '81, on 12 March, in an isolated village
in Siberia near the Lena River; my mother and father were
both in exile for political reasons. Their names were well-
known in their day, but are now forgotten: Victoria Saltykof
and the terrorist M . . . Maxime Davidovitch M . . .

I barely knew my father: prison and exile do not lend
themselves to a close-knit family. He was a tall man, with

shining, narrow eyes, dark eyebrows, and large, bony hands with delicate wrists. He rarely spoke. He had a sad, scathing little laugh. When they came to arrest him the last time, I was still a child. He hugged me, looked at me with a kind of ironic surprise, moved his lips slightly in a tired way that could pass for a smile, went out of the room, came back to get the cigarettes he'd forgotten, and disappeared for ever from my life. He died in prison, at about the age I am now, in a cell in the Pierre and Paul Fortress, where the waters from the Neva River had seeped in during the autumn floods.

After his arrest, I went to live in Geneva with my mother. I remember her better; she died in the spring of 1891. She was a delicate, slight creature, with fair hair and a pince-nez, the intellectual type of the '80s. I also remember her in Siberia, when we were going back, after she was freed. I was six years old. My brother had just been born.

She was holding him in her arms, but away from her chest, with extraordinary clumsiness, as if she were offering him to the stones along the road; she shivered as she listened to his hungry cries. Whenever she changed him, I could see her hands shaking and getting tangled up in the nappy and pins. She had beautiful, delicate, long hands. When she was sixteen, she'd killed the head of the Viatka police at point-blank range; he'd been torturing an old woman right in front of her, a political prisoner, forcing her to walk in the fierce heat of the Russian sun, even though she was ill. At the height of summer, the Russian sun batters you to death.

She told me about it herself, as if she felt she had to hurry, but before I was old enough to really understand. I remember the strange feeling I had listening to her story.

I remember her sounding resonant and shrill, different from the weary, patient tone of voice I was used to: 'I expected to be executed,' she said. 'I considered my death to be the supreme protest against a world of tears and bloodshed.'

She stopped for a moment. 'Do you understand, Logna?' she said more quietly. Her face and gestures remained cool and calm; only her cheeks had gone slightly red. She didn't wait for me to answer. My brother was crying. She got up, sighing, and picked him up. She held him for a moment, like a heavy package, then left us alone, and went back to coding her letters.

In Geneva, she was in charge of one of the Swiss terrorist groups, the same one that took care of me and raised me after she died. We lived on an allowance from the Party and from money she earned giving English and Italian lessons; we wore our winter clothes in Mont-de-Piété in springtime; summer clothes in autumn ... And so it went.

She was very tall and thin. She looked worn out at thirty, like an old woman; her hunched shoulders crushed her delicate chest. She suffered from tuberculosis, and her right lung was totally non-functional; but she would always say: 'How could I get medical care when the poor factory workers are coughing up blood?' (The revolutionaries of that generation always talked like that.) She didn't even send us away to live somewhere else: weren't the children of the workers infected by their own sick mothers?

However, I remember that she never kissed us. Besides, we were morose, cold children, at least I was. Only now and again, when she was very tired, would she stretch out her hand and stroke our hair, just once, slowly, as she sighed.

Her face was long and pale, with yellowish teeth and weary eyes that blinked behind her spectacles. She had delicate, clumsy hands that always dropped things in the house, that couldn't sew or cook, but wrote constantly, coding messages, forging passports ... I thought I had forgotten her features, what she looked like (so many years have passed by since then), but here they are, resurfacing once again in my memory.

Two or three nights a month, she would cross Lake Léman from Switzerland into France, carrying bundles of pamphlets and explosives. She would take me with her, perhaps to harden me to the dangerous life that was to be mine in years to come, in a kind of 'revolutionary dynastic tradition', perhaps to inspire trust in the customs officers, because I was so young, perhaps because my two brothers were dead and she didn't want to leave me alone in the hotel, the same way that middle-class mothers might take their children with them to the cinema. I would fall asleep on the deck. It was usually winter; the lake was deserted, covered in a thick fog; the nights were freezing cold. Once in France, my mother would leave me for a few hours with some farmers, the Bauds, who lived in a house beside the lake. They had six or seven children; I remember a group of little ruddy-cheeked kids, very healthy but very stupid. There I drank piping hot coffee. I ate warm bread with chestnuts. The Bauds' house, with its fires, the delicious aroma of coffee, the screaming children, was, to me, paradise on earth. They had a terrace, a sort of large wooden balcony that looked out over the lake, and, in winter, it was covered in snow and creaking ice.

I had two younger brothers; both had died. They'd also

lived alone in a hotel for a while, like me. One of them died when he was two, the other at three. I can particularly recall the night when the second one died; he was a good-looking boy, big and blond.

My mother was standing up, at the foot of the bed, an old bed made of dark wood. She held a lit candle in her hand and was watching the dying child. I was sitting on the floor beside her, and I could see her exhausted face, lit from below by the candle's flame. The child had one or two little convulsions, looked up with a weary, astonished expression, and died. My mother didn't move; her hand covering the flame was the only thing that was obviously trembling. Finally, she noticed me and wanted to say something (undoubtedly something like 'Logna, death is part of nature'), but she just clenched her lips sadly and said nothing. She placed the dead child on his pillow, took my hand and brought me to a neighbour's house. The silence, the darkness, and his pale face, his white nightshirt and long, fine blond hair, all this I remember as if it were a bewildering dream. Soon afterwards, she also died.

I was only ten years old then. I had inherited her predisposition to tuberculosis. The Revolutionary Committee lodged me at the home of Dr Schwann. A naturalised Swiss citizen of Russian origin, he was one of the leaders of the Party. He owned a private clinic that had twenty beds in Monts, near Sierre, and it was there that I lived. Monts is a bleak village between Montana and Sierre, buried between dark fir trees and gloomy mountains, or perhaps that's just how it seemed to me.

For years on end, I lived glued to a chaise-longue, on a balcony, seeing nothing of the world except the tops of the fir trees and, on the other side of the lake, a glass cage similar to ours that reflected the rays of the setting sun.

Later on, I was able to go out, down into the village, meeting the other patients along the only usable road. They were wrapped up in shawls, and we all climbed back together, breathing with difficulty, stopping after every few steps, counting the fir trees along the road, one by one, staring with hatred at the circle of mountains that shut out the sky. I can still see them, after all these years, just as I can smell the sanatorium, that odour of disinfectant and new linoleum, just as I can hear, in my dreams, the sound of the *föhn*, the dry autumn wind, in the forest.

With Dr Schwann, I studied foreign languages and medicine, which I particularly enjoyed. As soon as my health was better, I was given various assignments by the Revolutionary Committee in Switzerland and France.

I was a member of the Party by my very birth . . .

2

I began writing these notes thinking I would eventually write my autobiography. There's so much time to fill. You have to do something at the end of your life, one way or another. But already, here I am, stopping. 'A revolutionary education is difficult to explain in a way that is both sincere and instructive,' I recall that brave Hertz once said. And my code name, 'Léon M', has its place in the iconography of the October Revolution, which no doubt should be left intact. The son of parents living in exile, brought up exclusively on revolutionary speeches, tracts and models; and in spite of it all, I lacked strength and passion.

When I lived in Geneva, I would listen with envy as my friends talked about their youth. I recall a young man of thirty who had taken part in fourteen terrorist attacks, of which four had been successful; four of these murders had been carried out in vicious cold blood, in the middle of the street. He was a pale red-head with small, delicate, sweaty hands. One December evening after a meeting of the Committee, when we were coming back along the peaceful, frozen streets of Geneva, he told me how he had run away from home at the age of sixteen and wandered the streets of Moscow for eighteen days.

'What you never did,' he said, smiling, 'was to make your mother die of grief . . . or read illegal tracts by the light of a fire, like I did, when I was fifteen, at night, stretched out on the riverbank, in May . . .'

He spoke in a bizarre, rasping voice, in little rapid, breathless phrases, and sometimes he would stop and say with a sigh: 'The good old days . . .'

So true . . .

Later on, I also experienced exile, prison, the bunkers of the Pierre and Paul jail, the tiny cells, putrid-smelling in the summer heat, where twenty or thirty of us were locked up together; the vast, dark, freezing-cold prisons in the countryside and the fortress where those condemned to death were held and where it was possible, by pressing your ear to certain places in the wall, to hear the echo of revolutionary songs coming from the women's section.

But even now, I no longer appreciate the romantic side of the Revolution as much as I should.

An autobiography? Vanity. It would be better for me to remember certain things only for myself, as I did in the past. When I was in the state prisons they allowed us to write in notebooks, but then they destroyed them as soon as they were full of stories and memories.

Would I even have had the time to finish an autobiography? So much has happened, so many years gone by . . . I feel death approaching with a sense of weariness, of indifference, that is unmistakable: the debates, the changes within the Party, everything I used to feel so passionate about, I'm tired of all of it. Even my body is tired. More and more often, I want to turn over to face the wall, close my eyes, and fall into the deepest, sweetest sleep, for ever.

3

And so I belonged to the Party through my birth, my childhood, through the conviction that a social revolution is inevitable, necessary and fair, as fair as anything to do with human affairs could ever be. My love of power attracted me to it as much as my desire for a certain kind of human affection that I lacked, and it was the only place that I found it.

I like people, the masses. Here, near Nice, I live in Lourié's house. It is a cube made of white stone, in the middle of a garden where no tree grows higher than a broomstick; the house is between two roads, one leading to Monaco and the other to the sea; you breathe in a fine dust here that is full of petrol and is finishing off my poor old lungs. I live alone; in the morning, an old woman comes in to clean the four empty rooms that make up my house; she prepares my food and leaves. But the sounds of life continue to surround me, and that is what I love, that is what pleases me, people, cars, tramways going by, quarrels, shouting, laughter ... fleeting silhouettes, the faces of strangers, conversations ... Below, behind the bare little garden, where six delicate, sinuous bushes have been planted that will grow into peach trees, almond trees, goodness knows what, there is a kind of little Italian bistro, with a player piano, and benches beneath an arbour. Working men, Italian, French, go there to drink.

At night, when they begin to walk up the twisting road that runs along the sea, I come out of the house; I sit down on the small low wall that separates the garden from the bistro; I listen to them. I watch them.

I can see the small square lit up by paper lanterns, the pale light reflected on their faces. They go home late. The rest of the night passes more quickly that way, thank goodness, for I cough and fall asleep only when it's morning. Why do I sit here looking at the flowers and the sea? I hate nature. I have only ever been happy in cities, those ugly, dirty cities with houses full of people, and on the streets in summer, when it's hot, where I walk by strange faces and weary bodies. These are the hours I wish to kill, when solitude and silence surge up, when the last of the cars are returning from Monte Carlo along the coast road. Since I became ill, I am overwhelmed by memories. Before, I used to work. But my work is finished now.

And so I began my life as a revolutionary at the age of eighteen; I was given several missions in the south of France; then I lived in Paris for a long time. In 1903, the Committee sent me to Russia. I was to kill the Minister of Education. It was after this event that I broke away from the terrorist section of the Party and joined T. After the Courilof affair I was condemned to death, but a few days before my execution, Alexis, the heir to the throne, was born, and I was saved by the amnesty granted. My sentence was commuted to hard labour for life. When I learned that I had been spared, I cannot recall feeling anything except profound indifference. In any case, I was ill, I was coughing up buckets of blood, and I was sure to die on the way to Siberia. But you should never count on death any more than you should count on life.

I lived and was cured in Siberia, in the penal colony. When I escaped, the Revolution of 1905 had started.

Even though I was so exhausted at night that I would collapse and fall asleep as if I were dying, I have happy memories of 1905 and those first months of the Revolution.

I would go with R and L to the factories, to the workers' meetings. I have always had a piercing, unpleasant-sounding voice, and my weak lungs prevented me from speaking out loud for long. As for the others, they would rant at the workers for hours on end. I would leave the platform and mix with the crowd, explaining whatever they found confusing, advising them, helping them. Amid the heat and smoke in the room, their pale faces, their sparkling eyes, the shouts coming from their open mouths, their anger, even their stupidity, gave me the same feeling of euphoria you get from wine. And I liked the danger. I liked the sudden silences, how they held their breath in anticipation, the look of panic on their faces when they saw the *dvornik*, the informer who was in the pay of the police, walking past the window.

Into the dark night, those damp, freezing autumn nights in St Petersburg, the workers would leave, one by one. They melted into the fog like shadows. We would disappear after they had gone; to throw the police off the trail, we would roam the streets until dawn, stopping only when we reached the dirty little *traktirs* where we hid.

I left Russia only to return on the eve of the October Revolution. I have described this period and the one that followed in my previous writings on politics and history.

After 1917, I became the Bolshevik, Léon M. In newspapers all over the world, they must have depicted me wearing a helmet on my head and with a knife between my teeth. I was given a job in the Tcheka Secret Police, where I remained for one year. But it requires fierce, personal hatred to carry out such terrible work without flinching. As for me . . .

What is truly strange is that I, who spared not only innocent lives but several guilty ones as well (for at certain moments I was overcome by a kind of indifference, and the prisoners reaped the benefits), was hated even more than some of my comrades. For example, I was hated more than Nostrenko, the frenzied sailor who executed the prisoners himself; he was an extraordinary show-off who wore make-up and powder and left his shirt open exposing a chest as smooth and white as a woman's. I can still see him, a combination of bad actor, drunkard and pederast. Or Ladislas, the hunchback Pole, with his drooping, scarlet lip, slashed and scarred from an old wound.

I think the prisoners condemned to death vaguely consoled themselves with the idea that they were dealing with madmen or monsters; whereas I was an ordinary, sad little man who coughed, wore glasses, had a little snub nose and delicate hands.

When the policies of the leaders changed, I was sent into exile. Since then I have lived near Nice, supported by the modest income from books, newspaper articles, Party magazines. I ended up in Nice because I am living under the passport of a certain Jacques Lourié, who died of typhus in the Pierre and Paul Fortress, imprisoned for revolutionary conspiracy. He was a Jew from Latvia, a naturalised French citizen. He had no family, he was utterly alone, and he owned a small villa which I consequently inherited, as it were. The danger of running into his friends or neighbours pleased me somewhat. But everyone had forgotten Jacques Lourié. I live here, and will probably soon die here.

The house is small and not very comfortable, and Lourié, who was short of money, didn't have the walls surrounding it built high enough to stop people looking in.

On the left, there is a kind of enclosure, a piece of land for sale where goats come to graze on the thick sweet-smelling grass, between the abandoned bricks and stones. To the right, there is another little stone building, just like mine but painted pink, that is rented out to different couples each year. The road from Nice to Monte Carlo runs behind the house; below is the viaduct. The sea is far away. The house is cool and bright.

So this is how I live, and, sometimes, I don't know whether this tranquillity makes me happy or is killing me. Sometimes I feel I'd like to work again. At five o'clock, the time when my day used to begin in Russia, I wake with a start; or, if I haven't yet gone to sleep, I feel a profound sense of anguish. I pick up the odd thing: a book, a notebook. I write, as I am doing now. The weather is beautiful, the sun is rising, the roses smell wonderful. I would give it all, and my whole life, for that room where we all used to sleep, fifteen, twenty men, in 1917, when we came to power. It was a foggy night, snowing. You could hear the wind, the bombs, the faint sound of the Neva rising as it did every autumn. The telephone rang continuously. Sometimes I think: 'If I were younger and stronger, I would go back to Russia, I would start again, and I would die happy and at peace . . . in one of those prison cells I know so well.'

Power, the illusion of influencing human destiny, is as intoxicating as smoke, as wine. When you have none, you feel an astonishing sense of suffering, of painful uneasiness. At other times, as I've said, I feel nothing more than indifference and a sort of relief in remaining here and waiting for death to wash over me in a great wave. I am not suffering. It is only at night, when my fever rises, that a painful restlessness sweeps through my body, and the steady sound of my heart-beat echoes in my ears and tires me. By morning it has gone. I light the lamp, and I sit at my table, in front of the open window, and when the sun has finally risen, I fall asleep.

4

The Executive Committee in Switzerland met once a year to examine a list of dignitaries, senior civil servants in the Russian Empire renowned for their cruelty and injustice, and to choose who was to die that year. My mother had belonged to this organisation which, in my day, was made up of about twenty people.

In 1903, the Russian Minister of Education was Valerian Alexandrovitch Courilof, who was universally despised. He was a reactionary from the Pobiedonostsef school; he had a reputation as a man who exercised brute, cold-blooded force. Though protected by Emperor Alexander III and Prince Nelrode, he didn't belong to the nobility and, as often happens, was 'more of a royalist than the King'; he hated the Revolution and despised the ordinary people even more than the country's ruling classes.

He was tall and heavy, slow in his speech and movements; the students had nicknamed him the Killer Whale ('deadly and bloodthirsty'), for he was cruel, ambitious and hungry for military honours. He was enormously feared.

The leaders of the Party wanted him to be assassinated

in public, in the most grandiose manner possible, in order to catch the imagination of the people as much as possible. For this reason, this execution presented even greater difficulties than usual. Indeed, it was not enough to trust luck and throw a bomb, or shoot him, as we did, more or less, on most other occasions; in this case, we had to choose the right time and place. It was Dr Schwann who first spoke to me about this man. Schwann, when I knew him, must have been about sixty years old; he was short, slim, frail, and as light as a ballerina; his woolly hair, frizzy, completely white as milk or the moon, spilled over his forehead. He had a small, angular face, a tight mouth with a narrow, cruel shape, a delicate nose, as pinched and curved as a beak. He was mad. He was declared so officially, so to speak, only after I left, and he died in an asylum in Lausanne. However, even at this earlier time, he already aroused within me an instinctive sense of foreboding and revulsion. He was something of a genius: he had been one of the first to experiment on pneumothorax in tuberculosis. He enjoyed destroying and healing in equal measures.

I can still picture him on my balcony, with me, a twelve-year-old child stretched out and wrapped up in my fur blanket, the moon illuminating the pine trees, the snow blue and thick, the frozen little lake sparkling in the shadows. The moonlight bathed Schwann's halo of white hair, his strange dressing gown with its pink and baby-blue pattern, as he taught me the terrorist doctrine:

'Logna, you see a gentleman like that one over there, big, fat, who's bursting, feeding on the blood and sweat of the people . . . You laugh. You think: "Wait, just you wait." He doesn't know you. You are there, in the shadows.

You start to move . . . like this . . . you raise your hand
. . . a bomb isn't very big, you know; you can hide it in
a shawl, in a bouquet of flowers . . . Whoosh! . . . It
explodes! The gentleman is blown up, flesh and bones
flying in all directions.'

He spoke in a whisper, interspersed with laughter.

'And his soul will also fly away . . . *animula vagula,
blandula* . . . little soul, wandering soul.' (He was obsessed
with Latin quotations, just like poor Courilof.)

He entwined his fingers in the most bizarre fashion, as
if he were plaiting hair; his little hooked nose, his pinched
mouth, were outlined with the sharpness of steel against
the bluish, silvery background of the pine trees, the snow
and the moon.

One of the Party leaders sometimes gave him large sums
of money, I've never understood how. Some people believe
he'd also been an agent provocateur, but I don't think so.

He was the one who took me along to the Executive
Committee meeting in 1903. It was a cold and glistening
winter's night. We made our way to Lausanne on the little
milk train that creaked as it descended the steep frozen
fields, as hard and brittle as salt. We were alone in the
compartment; Schwann was wrapped up in a shepherd's
greatcoat, wearing no hat, as usual, despite the cold.

There, in his low murmur, he spoke to me again of the
Killer Whale.

Twice already, the Committee had sent men to kill the
minister, but both of them had been arrested and hung.
The Committee had recognised that it would be almost
impossible for Russians to carry out the assassination. The
police knew all the suspects; no matter how well disguised

they might be, they couldn't hide their true identity for long; their arrests would compromise the work of the other Party members and would mean their death.

Moreover, for a while now, terrorist attacks had been kept secret; even the foreign press hardly mentioned them. This assassination had to take place audaciously, as I've already mentioned, where the people could see it with their own eyes. And insofar as possible, it had to be witnessed by the ambassadors of foreign governments, somewhere in public, during an official ceremony or on a public holiday, which made it ten times more difficult. As for me, well, nobody knew me, not the police, not the Russian revolutionaries. I spoke Russian, although with a heavy foreign accent, which was not necessarily a bad thing; it would therefore be easy to get me into the country with a Swiss passport.

I listened to Schwann speak, though it is difficult for me, with so many years' distance, to remember exactly what I felt. The Committee had a reputation for justice; it condemned only people who were guilty of crimes. And the conviction that I was risking my own life as much as the minister was risking his, this conviction was the justification for the murder and absolved me of it. Also, I was only twenty-two years old. I was nothing like the man I was to become. All I knew of life was a sanatorium and a dingy little room in Montrouge. I was eager, thirsty, for life; already I enjoyed the feeling of holding someone's life in my hands, the way you might hold a live bird.

I said nothing to Schwann. I tapped the window where the snow had stuck to it. I looked outside. Soon, we came to the plain where the fir trees grew scarcer; through the darkness you could see their branches sparkling, heavy with ice, lit up by the first log fires.

Finally, we arrived in Lausanne, where the Committee was meeting that night.

I knew all the Committee members, but it was the first time I'd ever seen them all together. There was Loudine and his wife, Roubakof, Brodsky, Dora Eisen, Leonidif, Hertz . . . Most of them, since then, have died a violent death.

A few of them, on the other hand, gave up just in time. Hertz is still living here in France. When I came to Nice, I ran into him once on the Promenade des Anglais, strolling arm in arm with his wife, walking a little dog with curly white hair; he looked old and ill, but peaceful, just like a good little member of the French bourgeoisie.

He walked past without recognising me. It was on his orders that General Rimsky and Minister Bobrinof had been killed.

In 1907, he was supposed to blow up the Emperor's train, but he made a mistake and ordered the bomb to be thrown under the Petersburg–Yalta train, while the Emperor and his family were travelling in the opposite direction. It was a mistake that cost the lives of twenty-odd people (not counting the men who had followed his orders, thrown the bomb, and didn't have time to get away: such are the risks of the profession).

The meeting of the Committee in 1903 took place in Loudine's room; it lasted barely an hour. In order to confuse the neighbours, some wine bottles had been placed on a table, lit up by a lamp, opposite the window. Now and again, one of the women would get up and play some waltzes on an old piano in the corner of the room. I was given a passport in the name of Marcel Legrand, born in Geneva, a doctor of medicine, diplomas as proof of my qualifications, and some money. Then everyone went back home, while I checked into a hotel.

5

I can remember in extraordinary detail the room where I spent that night. Through the old threadbare carpet, I could see floorboards the colour of rope; I paced up and down all night as if in a trance. A small cloudy mirror, above the sink, reflected the image of the dark wooden furniture, the green wallpaper, and my pale, anxious face. I remember opening the window. I forced myself to look at a small, grey church, streaked with soft snow. Here and there, on the deserted street, gloomy lights were burning. I felt unspeakably exhausted and miserable. Throughout my entire life, just before I was about to do something essential to the fate of my Party – I'm not talking about my own life, which has never really been of much interest to me – I have always felt overwhelmed by deadly indifference. The clean, cold air finally brought me back to life. And, little by little, the secret exultation I had felt in the train won me over once again, the realisation that I was going to leave this lethal place, that I was cured, that the life of a revolutionary, with its passions and battles, was there waiting for me, and so many other things as well . . . I remained at the hotel for a few days.

Finally, one morning, 25 January 1903, I received my

orders and left. I was to go to Kiev, and once there, my first order of business was to make myself known to a woman called Fanny Zart, who would follow me to St Petersburg and help me. When I left Lausanne, something strange happened, something that struck me, and, even though it was insignificant and never had anything to do with my own life afterwards, I have never forgotten it. Even now, I still have dreams about it.

That day I had gone to Monts for one last meeting with Dr Schwann and was returning to Lausanne on a little train, slowly puffing away, that stopped at each and every station. I was meant to reach Lausanne at midnight. We arrived in Vevey around ten o'clock in the evening. The station appeared deserted and you could even hear a little bell ringing in the total silence.

Suddenly, on the platform opposite me, I saw a man running towards a train that was pulling into the station. Schwann and I were walking by. The man looked like he wanted to throw himself under the train. A woman, standing next to me, let out a sharp little cry. All of a sudden, I saw him spin around, in a kind of circle, like a bird gliding downwards; he threw himself to the ground, then got up, started running again and fell over in exactly the same way – two or three times, he did this. Finally, he stayed on the ground, his body twitching.

The train had stopped; the passengers saw what was happening, jumped out, and helped the man up. I could see them lean over him, asking him questions, but he said nothing, just waved his arms in an astonished, feeble gesture, then began to sob uncontrollably.

They sat him down on a bench, stared at him for a

moment, then left him there: the train was about to leave. I have carried the image of that man with me ever since: sitting, alone, in the deserted train station, on a cold January night, a big man in mourning, with a thick black moustache, a black felt hat, large hands clutching his knees in desperate resignation.

Afterwards, I often wondered why that incident made such a strong impression on me, for the face of that big man haunted me for years, it's true, and in my dreams, I watched his features merge with the Killer Whale's, after his murder. They looked a little like each other.

In Kiev, I found the address I'd been given for the medical student, Fanny Zart. She was a young woman of twenty, with a stocky build and black hair pulled forward over her cheeks like great sideburns; she had a long straight nose, a strong mouth whose lower lip drooped and gave her face an obstinate and scornful expression. Her eyes were unique to women in the Party, eyes whose harshness and determination were inhuman. (Only those of the second generation, nothing like the weary, short-sighted look of my mother.) She was the daughter of a watchmaker in Odessa and the sister of an extremely wealthy banker in St Petersburg who financed her education and wanted nothing more to do with her. Because of this, her hatred of the wealthy classes took the concrete form of this little Jewish banker with his fat stomach. She had been a member of the Party for three years.

In Kiev, she lived in one large room on the top floor of a corner house; from her window, you could see both the market and the town square and, past the square, a long, deep road that ended at a charming gilded church.

Afterwards, once we'd taken Kiev, I remembered that house: I had machine guns installed in it; when the people of Makhno came out of the church and filled the town square, pillaging and killing, we mowed them down.

She gave me a passport that belonged to one of her brothers: it had been agreed that the name Marcel Legrand would be used only in St Petersburg, to cover my tracks as thoroughly as possible.

That very evening, I moved in with her. I was alone almost all day long. She was studying at the university, and when she got home at night she would make us something to eat, and we would talk; or rather, she would talk, going over and over the list of people to be assassinated.

Heavy snow fell over the frozen town square: you could see the policemen going home in pairs. Kiev was a small provincial town then, peaceful and dismal. Never have I seen, anywhere else, such beautiful sunsets, mournful and dazzling. The sky on the western side suddenly turned blood-red and hazy with purplish smoke. Endless flocks of crows flew about until nightfall, deafening us with their cries, with the beating of their wings. From our windows, we could see the houses all lit up, peaceful silhouettes behind the window-panes, the flickering light of paraffin lamps set on the floors in the shops, giving off a smoky glow all around them.

I saw no one but Fanny; according to the instructions I'd received, I was to meet no one else in the Party. Perhaps the leaders in Geneva were already beginning to suspect A of being a traitor.

Finally, I left Kiev with Fanny. We arrived in St Petersburg the day before Easter.

6

I went to a boarding-house she recommended to me; it was run by a Madame Schröder, a woman of German descent who had started out running a brothel that she later turned into a hotel with furnished rooms. She worked for both the revolutionaries and the police. Due to a kind of reciprocal tolerance, these types of places were the safest.

Streams of prostitutes came there; they were unknowingly our free informers. In the evening, before going back to the Nevsky River or the cabarets, they met up at Schröder's place; we'd put a pitcher of vodka or some tea on the table and they would give us, without even realising it, names and addresses better than any professional revolutionary could. They were kind creatures, sweet and totally penniless. They were reactionaries at heart, like most prostitutes usually are, and never suspected the role they were made to play by both sides. At least that was the case with most of them; certain amongst them knowingly betrayed others for money, out of jealousy or because they loved talking.

The next day was Easter Sunday. The very night we arrived, we decided to go to Saint Isaac's Cathedral, where, according to Fanny's informants, Courilof would be attending mass. This way, I could see what the minister looked like in person, rather than from photos. Easter that year coincided with the commemoration of a saint whose name I have forgotten: for this reason, Courilof wouldn't sit in the ministers' chapel for mass, as he ordinarily did.

Fanny was going to point him out to me and would then disappear. She was suspected by the police: her name had been mixed up in some secret typography business. That was why the Party had refused to entrust her with carrying out the assassination. She was an extraordinarily intelligent and sharp woman, driven by a kind of nervous passion, a constant tension I have seen, to that level, only in women, a tension that made it possible for them to perform miracles of endurance and energy. Then, suddenly, they would collapse, and either kill themselves or cross over to the other side, selling us to our enemies. Many of them, however, died courageously.

That same evening, Fanny had managed to get hold of some money and buy some second-hand peasant clothing so she could disguise herself. We took two large candles and *koulitch* cakes with us that could be blessed at church, and set off to take the longest route, so that Fanny could show me the ministerial palace where Courilof lived. St Petersburg seemed extraordinarily beautiful to me. Easter had fallen very late that year; the nights were already light.

You could clearly see the red palaces, the quaysides, the dark granite houses. I stopped in front of the ministry, stared for a long time at the columns, the wrought-iron balconies; the stonework was the same deep red of the state buildings, the colour of dried blood. High gates surrounded a garden that was still bare; through the naked branches, I could see a sandy courtyard, a wide staircase of white marble.

We headed back to Saint Isaac's. The streets were full of poor people, like us, who were holding candles and cakes wrapped in white cloth napkins. They were being sold from tables set up amidst the biting wind. Cars passed slowly by. We got to the town square, where the crowd waited. I saw members of the diplomatic corps go inside – ministers, important dignitaries, women – then we went in with the ordinary people, crossing ourselves as they did.

Fanny made her way forward to a hidden corner of the church from where we could see the first pews. The scent of smoke from the incense was so strong that my head started pounding, and I felt as if I were looking through a haze at a crowd of people in evening dress, sparkling uniforms decorated with ribbons and stars. Their faces, in the candlelight, looked yellow, like the faces of corpses, their mouths surrounded by deep shadows. The clergymen, gleaming, chanted and swung their incense burners towards us.

'Third from the row on the left, between two women,' said Fanny. 'One woman has a bird of paradise on her hat, the other's young, in a white dress.'

I looked, and through the wafting incense, I could see a large man, heavy, whose hair and eyebrows were nearly white, with a square, unkempt beard and an expression that was callous, haughty and stern. I studied him for a long time. He was as still as a stone. He raised his hand slowly to make the sign of the cross, but his enormous neck, his wide, powerful face, never moved; he didn't bat an eyelash. His wide, pale eyes stared straight ahead, fixed on the altar.

Fanny, holding a red handkerchief tightly to her chin, stared at him, her eyes burning. About a hundred policemen, some in uniform, some in civilian clothing but all unmistakable from their stiffness and their arrogant look of brutality, formed a barrier that separated this dazzling gathering of dignitaries and ministers from the masses.

The heat became so unbearable that I felt my temples throbbing; I could hear the muffled, wild beating of my heart. We knelt down like everyone around us, and the hymns seemed to crash down from the magnificent vaults above.

I couldn't see Courilof any more; I was overwhelmed by a feeling of feverish unreality; automatically, like the people around me, I bent down to touch my head to the floor. From the marble flagstones, a cold breeze, smelling frozen and damp, wafted upwards.

Finally, the service ended. We went outside; the police held the masses back; I saw Courilof get into a car, helped by a lackey in a black hat decorated with the official state emblem.

The clergy walked around the church three times; you could see the icons' long ribbons softly undulating in the clear night. Three times the priests passed by, holding up the sparkling cross, and their chants faded away into the distance.

We broke away from the crowd and followed the Nevsky River back to my house. Like everyone else, we were holding lit candles; the perfume from the wax filled the air; they burned with tall, high, transparent flames, for the night was very warm, without a hint of a breeze. 'Symbol of peace, symbol of happiness,' said some women behind us as they cupped their hands around the bright flames. Above our heads, the sky began to darken, but the horizon remained clear and pink, casting pale shadows and shimmering reflections over the water in the canals.

Once again, we passed by the gates of the ministry; it was still open, and cars were going inside to the gardens. We could clearly see women in ball gowns through the windows and hear the faint sound of music playing. The entire house was lit up from top to bottom.

I don't know why, but walking along that street, feeling sick (the smell of the incense and the heat in the church had made me nauseous and feverish), I thought of the minister's impassive, hostile face and felt, for the first time in my life, a kind of hatred. My heart was filled with venom.

Curiously, Fanny seemed to sense how I felt.

'Well?' she said dryly, looking at me.

I shrugged my shoulders and didn't reply.

For the first time, this secretive and proud young woman told me about herself, her life story. We were sitting on one of those benches carved out of granite along the quayside. The wind from the Neva River was blowing, still crisp and heavy with the smell of ice; it blew out our candles.

Since then, I have heard many of our women tell the same story; their lives were all similar with their wounded pride, their yearning for freedom and vengeance. But there was something affected and overly enthusiastic in her words and voice that troubled me and froze me to the core. She was obviously upset; her eyes sought mine with a kind of goodwill, the desire to move me, to fill me with pity, admiration and horror. I was barely listening to her: that entire night was like a nightmare, and her words merged into the surreal confusion of a feverish dream.

7

I spent a month keeping close watch at the villa, trying in vain to find a way to get inside. Little by little, I began to feel passionately excited; day and night I prowled around that house, questioning delivery men, the minister's lowliest employees, talkative shopkeepers in the neighbourhood. Within a short time, I knew Courilof's superficial life, his habits, the days and times he went to see the Emperor, the names of his friends, what ordinary people thought of him. Savage, ambitious: these words continually came up. I learned that he had lost his first wife, who came from an influential family protected by the Emperor's mother. She had favoured Courilof's rise to power; since Nicolas had ascended to the throne, Prince Alexander Alexandrovitch Nelrode had become the minister's protector.

Courilof had a son and a daughter from his first marriage, who lived with him; the boy was still a child and the girl was old enough to be married. About a year earlier, he had finally married his French mistress, Margot, a woman of dubious morals. Her real name was Marguerite Darcy; she was a former actress with a comic opera company and with whom Courilof had had a long-standing affair dating back to his youth.

One day, I saw this woman coming out of the house with the minister's daughter. I recognised the two women who had been sitting on either side of Courilof in the cathedral. The young woman was petite, with an extremely girlish face, almost childlike, with brown hair, pale, delicate, very pretty, and wide blue eyes; as for the woman . . . she was an extraordinary creature. She looked like an ageing bird of paradise: fading, losing its brilliant plumage, but still as dazzling as costume jewellery, the kind they wear in the theatre. She wore far too much make-up; the midday sun ruthlessly highlighted the pink stains on her cheeks, the fine but deep little wrinkles in her skin. Her face must have grown fuller with the passing years, but thanks to the pure lines of certain features, you could still see that she must have once been very beautiful.

She passed by so closely that she knocked into me, then gathered up the folds of her lace skirt and looked at me. Her eyes, so close to mine, astonished me with their beauty. Very dark, sparkling, edged with thin, black eyelashes, they had an intense, weary expression that struck me. She reminded me of an old prostitute I'd known at Schröder's, a complete wreck, who had that same intense, weary look.

She muttered a few words of apology in a strong French accent (her voice was affected and unpleasant) and kept walking. I followed her for a while. She had a ridiculous walk; she bounced like many old actresses do, as if they're afraid they'll make the floor-boards of the stage creak because their legs have grown heavy with age.

'That woman,' Fanny told me later, 'lived with him openly for fourteen years. They held infamous orgies at their house in the Iles.'

I avoided being there when the minister himself came out. I didn't want to attract the attention of his informers who, especially when he was going to see the Emperor, seemed to surface from every nook and cranny of the city and head for his house, as if their goal was to point out his presence to the whole neighbourhood. Later on, I found out that ministers who were somewhat in disfavour were kept under surveillance in this obviously tactless way; but at the time it surprised me.

Only once did I spot Courilof, and it was almost by accident. I was involuntarily drawn to his neighbourhood and house. I was walking past his front door when I saw, from the corner, that he was about to come out; the doorman and policemen were standing even more to attention than usual, their faces attentive and stern. Here and there, on the street corners, policemen in civilian clothing paced back and forth. (I'd learned how to recognise them: of all the inhabitants of St Petersburg, they were the only ones who wore bowler hats and carried big rolled-up umbrellas, summer and winter alike.)

The door opened and Courilof headed for his car, followed by his secretary. He walked quickly and frowned, a sullen, dark expression on his face. I backed against a wall and watched him. Then, as strange as it may seem, he turned and looked at me, just as his wife had, but he seemed to look through me, without seeing me. It came to me in a flash that, to him, I was the living form Death had taken on this earth, and also – he was so fat, so impassive and solemn – I would take pleasure in seeing this superbly decorated mass, that harsh face explode into 'flesh and bones flying in all directions'. At that moment, I hated him – as I had hated Dr Schwann in the past – with a feeling that was almost physical. I looked away and he walked past, continuing along. I went and sat down in a little cabaret where I had something to eat and remained for part of the night.

The next day, Fanny told me that sixty students had been arrested on charges of revolutionary activities at the insistence of the minister. One of the history professors had refused to answer their questions about the Paris Commune. These young people had protested in the only way they could, a stupid and childish way, smashing up their desks and singing revolutionary songs at the top of their voices (the 'International' and the 'Marseillaise' jumbled together), during the service in the chapel. Soldiers had cleared out the lecture halls.

I dined at Madame Schröder's place where she talked to me about Courilof's wife; she'd known her when she was twenty, 'when she sang "Giroflé-Girofla" in the little cabarets on the Iles. Afterwards, she became Prince Nelrode's mistress before meeting His Excellency.'

'Does Courilof know that the prince received the lady's favours before him?' I asked.

But Madame Schröder told me that this circumstance, for some unknown reason, had made them even closer. She was still talking when Fanny came in, to tell us that in the city soldiers had opened fire and several young men and women had been wounded and killed. I have never seen, on a human face, a greater look of hatred than I saw on Fanny's face that day; her green eyes were blazing. Even I was deeply moved.

When we left, the city was utterly silent, as if it had been crushed. Several times since then I have experienced that extraordinary silence: it is the most definite sign that a revolution is about to begin. On that particular night, there were a few small revolts in the factories and textile works, immediately suppressed with extreme violence.

We walked through almost the entire city, hearing nothing except the sound of iron shutters quickly closing in front of the shops. Only a few remained open; a single lantern placed on the ground faintly lit them up.

The gates were closed in front of the great rectangular courtyard of the university, but just as we were arriving, a small group of men carrying stretchers went inside. We slipped in behind them and the gates shut again. The university buildings were as dark as night. Suddenly a light shone from one of the rooms; you could see it through the tall windows of the lecture halls shimmering faintly in the clear night. I don't know why, but it looked inexplicably sinister.

We hid behind the high columns and remained there, motionless, spellbound, in spite of the very real danger, for the police continually rushed past us.

On the other side of the street, the houses were locked and dark. Just as we were about to leave, blending in with people who were coming and going, a car sped past and we recognised Courilof.

One of the guards went over to open the car door for him, but Courilof gestured that he wasn't getting out. They exchanged a few words; even though I was quite close to them, I couldn't make out anything. In the moonlight, as pure and clear as the rising sun, I could see the tall, motionless shape of the minister; his face was so cold and harsh that it didn't even look human.

At that moment, we heard footsteps coming from inside the courtyard and the men carrying the stretchers came out. There were eight of them, I think. As they passed in front of the car, they stopped and pulled back the sheets.

A man was standing next to Courilof; I can still picture him, short and pale with a big yellowish moustache and a nervous tic that made his upper lip twitch. He wrote down the names of the victims on a register as the stretcher bearers handed him notebooks, identity papers, passports, all undoubtedly found in the victims' clothes.

For a second, I could see their young faces, their closed eyes, and that unforgettable look of secret, profound scorn that corpses have a few hours after they die, when the traces of suffering and terror have faded.

They were carried over to a parked black van and thrown in with a dull grunt, the kind porters make when they're lifting heavy trunks.

The minister made a gesture and the policemen stood back to let the car speed out. I had just enough time to see the minister lean back in the corner and pull his hat down over his eyes. I have never lost the impression of intense horror I felt at that sight.

8

I had thought about trying to get myself into the minister's house by posing as a French valet, a tutor or a doctor. It was this final choice that prevailed. One of our members in the Swiss delegation recommended me to his superior, who, in all innocence, recommended me to Courilof. Every year when Courilof went to stay in his house in the Iles, and then to the Caucasus, he took a young doctor, preferably foreign, along with him.

I went to the embassy and, with my false passport and letters of recommendation, I managed to achieve my goal more quickly than the real Marcel Legrand might have done. I obtained a letter from the Swiss minister, who guaranteed I was politically sound; the same day, I went to the ministry. There I was received by a secretary who examined my papers and kept them; then he asked me to come back the next day, which I did.

And so there I was the next day, waiting.

Courilof quickly lumbered across the room to shake my hand. I was struck by how different his features appeared when seen close up, compared to how I remembered them. He seemed older, and his face, which in public was as impassive as a block of marble, now looked flabbier, more mottled, softer, made of whitish fat; he had dark circles under his eyes.

I had noticed, the day when we crossed paths near his house, the way he had looked me in the eye without appearing to actually see me, as if he were looking for something behind a glass wall. His forehead and ears seemed enormous. Throughout the few seconds our meeting lasted, I could feel his weary blue eyes staring at me. Later on, I was told that it was a tic of Alexander III, this serious way of staring at someone without blinking. Undoubtedly, the minister was imitating him. But most significantly, he looked as if he were obsessed with one particular idea; beneath his distracted, fixed gaze, it wasn't fear that you felt, but rather annoyance and confusion.

He asked me a few questions, then asked if I could move into their house in the Iles the following Monday.

'I'll be there for the month of June,' he said, 'then in the Caucasus in autumn . . .'

I agreed. He gestured to the secretary, who accompanied me to the door. I left.

The following Monday, I was driven to the Iles. Courilof's house was built at the very edge, in a place called La Flèche, which looked out over the entire coast of Finland; here, the setting sun shimmered all night long during the month of May, bathing everything in its brilliant silvery light. Thin birch trees and miniature firs grew in the spongy soil, full of dark, stagnant water. Never have I seen so many mosquitoes. In the evening, a whitish mist settled around the houses as thick clouds of them flew in from the marshes.

The houses in the Iles were very beautiful. Sometimes, a villa in Nice reminds me of Courilof's villa, for it was built in the same Italian style, pompous and rococo, the stonework the colour of saffron with foundation walls painted sea green and adorned with great, bow-shaped balconies.

During the civil war, the entire villa was destroyed. I went back there once, I recall, during the 19 October battles against Youdenitch, when I was chief administrator of the army. Our Red Army was camping along the coast. I could find no trace of the house, it had been completely destroyed by the shells. It seemed to have been swallowed up by the earth; water had sprung up everywhere; it was virtually a pond, deep and calm, where you could hear the piercing buzz of those mosquitoes . . . Breathing in the smell of that water gave me a strange sensation.

I lived in that house for a while: it was me, Courilof's son Ivan, who was ten years old, and his Swiss tutor, Froelich. The minister had been delayed by the Emperor. Then Courilof's wife and daughter Ina (Irène Valerianovna) arrived, and finally the minister himself.

9

Valerian Alexandrovitch Courilof arrived one night, quite late. I was already in bed. The sound of the car along the cobblestones in the courtyard woke me up.

I went over to the window. The servants were still holding the car door open as Courilof got out, helped by a secretary; he seemed to be having trouble walking and he crossed the courtyard with slow, heavy steps that pounded the ground. When he reached the stairs, he stopped, pointed to his luggage, and gave some orders I couldn't make out. I watched him. At that point in time, I never grew weary of watching him . . . I think that fishermen who have waited patiently for a very long time at the river's edge and finally feel their line bend and tremble in their hands, then reel in their salmon or sterling, must have the same feeling as they contemplate their dazzling catch twitching and sparkling at their feet.

Courilof had been inside the house for a long time, yet I stood there for a long time, feverishly dreaming of the moment when I would see him dead by my hand.

That night, I didn't go back to bed; I was reading when a servant came in.

'Come downstairs at once,' he said. 'His Excellency isn't well.'

I went down to the minister's bedroom. As I got closer to the door, I heard a voice barely recognisable as Courilof's, a kind of continuous cry, interspersed with groans and sighs: 'My God! My God! My God! . . .'

'Hurry up,' the servant urged. 'His Excellency is very bad.'

I went in. The room was in total disorder. I saw Courilof stretched out on his bed, completely naked; a candle lit up his fat, yellowish body. He was thrashing around from side to side, undoubtedly trying to find a position that wasn't painful; but every movement caused him to cry out in anguish. When he saw me, he started to speak but suddenly a flood of dark vomit shot out of his mouth. I looked at his yellow cheekbones, the harsh circles under his narrowed eyes. He pointed to the region near his liver; his hand was shaking as he watched me, his large eyes wide open. I tried to examine it, but his abdominal wall was covered in fat; nevertheless, I noticed the abnormal thinness of his ribcage and legs in contrast to his enormous stomach.

His wife, kneeling behind him, was holding his head in both hands.

'His liver?' I asked.

She nodded towards a syringe of morphine on the table that had been prepared for him.

'Professor Langenberg normally looks after His Excellency, but he's away,' she murmured.

I injected the morphine and put hot compresses over the area around his liver. Courilof fell into a fitful sleep, interspersed with groans.

I kept changing the compresses for nearly an hour. He had stopped groaning, but sighed deeply every now and then. There was no hair at all on his body, but it was covered in a whitish fat, like wax. I noticed a little gold icon on his chest, hanging from his neck on a silk ribbon. The entire room – very large and dark, irregularly shaped, with dark green, almost black carpeting – was covered from top to bottom in images of the Virgin and saints, like a chapel. An enormous icon in a gold frame took up one entire corner of the room; it contained a statue of the Black Madonna – her hair was studded with gemstones, her face sorrowful and unattractive. The tapestries were lit up in places by little shimmering lights cast by the lamps in the icons; I counted three of them above the bed, lined up one on top of the other, in the folds of a billowing curtain.

His wife hadn't moved; she continued holding his rigid, yellowish head ever so carefully, as if he were a sleeping child. I told her she should leave him, as he was unconscious. She didn't reply, didn't even seem to hear me, just clasped his tilted head even more tightly. He was breathing with difficulty, his mouth open and nostrils dilated, his wide pale eyes burning beneath his lowered eyelids.

'Valia . . . my love; Valia, my darling . . .' she whispered.

I watched her closely. She looked exhausted; her face, free of make-up, was the face of an old woman . . . but she must have been beautiful once. She possessed an extraordinary mixture of the ridiculous and the pathetic. Her hair was arranged in little gold ringlets, like a child's; her mouth, lined with deep, fine wrinkles, looked like the tiny cracks found on paintings. Circles around her eyes formed a kind of dark ring near the sockets; perhaps it was this that gave her such a deep, weary expression.

'Do you think he's cold?' she murmured. 'When he's in pain like this, he can't even stand the feel of sheets on his body.'

I went to get a blanket and covered his naked body; he was starting to shake with cold and fever. I was being very gentle, but I couldn't help brushing against the area around his liver. He let out a kind of bestial moan, and, though I don't know why, it moved me.

'There, there,' I said. 'It's gone now.'

I put my hand on his forehead and wiped away the perspiration. My hands were cold and his forehead was burning hot. I knew it must have felt good to him. I slowly stroked his head and face again; I looked at him.

'Are you feeling better, Valia, my darling?' his wife said quietly.

'Leave him,' I said again. 'He's sleeping.'

She raised his head and carefully put it down on the pillow. I took a flask of vinegar, wet my hands, started stroking his face again. He lay stretched out in front of me; despite his suffering, his pale face retained its cold, harsh expression.

The servant had remained in the room, standing in a corner, dozing off. 'Should I go back and get Professor Langenberg?' he asked quietly.

'Yes, do,' said Madame Courilof quickly. 'Hurry, hurry up.'

I went over to the open window and sat down on the ledge where I could smoke and breathe more comfortably. It was already morning and the first cars were driving past.

A while later, Courilof sat up and gestured for me to come over.

'They've gone to get Professor Langenberg,' I said.

'Thank you. You did a good job. You seem to know what you're doing.'

He spoke to me in French, in a gentle, emotional tone of voice. He must have been suffering horribly; his face was grey and he had dark circles under his eyes. His wife leaned over him; she stroked his cheek gently and remained standing next to his bed, watching him carefully.

He told me I could examine him; I did so very gently and when he asked me questions, I told him I thought he'd been working too hard. I was struck by the terrible condition in which I found almost all of his organs. He looked as if he were made of steel, and his demeanour, his girth, his height, made him look like a giant. However, his lungs were congested, his heart-beat irregular and quick; there wasn't a single muscle beneath this mass of flesh.

I carefully returned to the area around his liver; I thought I could feel an abnormal growth, but he stopped me, growing even paler: 'Don't, please,' he said.

He pointed to the right side of his body. 'Here, over here. There's a sharp pain, like someone's cutting me with a razor.'

The way he'd moved had obviously caused him more pain. He groaned, angrily clenching his teeth: he was so accustomed to controlling everything with certain gestures, a certain look, that he unconsciously used the same methods when dealing with illness and death.

A little while later, he seemed calmer and started talking

again. He spoke quietly, said his life was difficult and that he felt very tired. He sighed several times, waving his large hand about. It was shaking slightly.

'You don't understand, you don't know this country, but we're going through hard times,' he said. 'Everyone's authority has been weakened. People loyal to the Emperor have a heavy burden to bear.'

The longer he spoke, the more he began to use pompous and affected language. There was a strange contrast between his moralistic words and the old, weary expression on his face, where you could still see tears in his eyes from the pain he was suffering.

He stopped talking. 'Go and get some rest, Marguerite,' he whispered to his wife.

She gave him a long kiss on the forehead and went out.

I followed her, and as I walked past her, I looked at her face with curiosity.

'He has a problem with his liver . . . doesn't he?' she asked with a look of fear and anguish on her exhausted face.

'Undoubtedly.'

She hesitated, then said quietly: 'You'll see, that Langenberg . . . These doctors, these Russians, I don't trust them . . . If he weren't a minister, things would certainly be very different! But they hide behind each other so no one takes any responsibility. They're afraid, they're never around when you need them!'

She spoke quickly, in a guttural Parisian accent, half swallowing her words. She shook her odd-looking golden hair, staring at me with wide, tired eyes. 'Are you French?'

'No, Swiss.'

'Ah!' she said. 'That's a shame.' She thought for a moment in silence. 'But . . . you do know Paris?' she finally asked.

'Yes.'

'I'm from Paris,' she said, looking at me with pride. And her eyes and teeth automatically lit up with a dazzling smile. 'I'm a Parisian!'

We'd reached the staircase. I stood back to let her pass; she gathered up her flowing robe, placed her foot on the first step – it was still pretty, shapely with a high arch, and she was wearing gold, high-heeled slippers. She was about to go up the stairs when a servant, who was walking through the hallway, dropped a tray full of porcelain.

I could clearly hear the shatter of crockery and the young girl's nervous, shrill scream. Madame Courilof, stiff and white as a sheet, seemed frozen to the spot. I tried to reassure her but she wasn't listening to me; she just stood there, pale and motionless. Only her lips quivered, turning her face into a grotesque grimace that was horrible to behold.

I opened the sitting-room door, pointed to the servant kneeling on the floor, cleaning up the shards of glass. Only then did a bit of colour return to her cheeks.

She sighed deeply and went upstairs without saying a word. On the landing, as we were parting, she forced herself to smile. 'I live under the constant threat of a terrorist attack,' she said to me. 'My husband is well respected by the people . . . but . . .'

She didn't finish her sentence, just lowered her head and walked quickly away. Later on, every time the minister was late, I would see her lean out the window, undoubtedly expecting to see a stretcher with a dead body on it being carried down the path. The sound of any unfamiliar foot-steps or voices in the house made her start in the same way; a deathly pallor would come over her face – the miserable expression of a hunted animal waiting for the deadly blow, but not knowing how or when it would come.

After the minister was assassinated, I can recall with perfect clarity hiding in the room next to where his body was laid out. When she came in, she looked almost at peace; her eyes were dry. She seemed free at last.

10

The next day, Courilof called me in while Langenberg was there.

Langenberg was a large man, Germanic looking and blond, with a sharp, square beard and a cold, ironic, piercing expression behind his spectacles. His cold, damp hands made Courilof's body shiver nervously when he touched him; I could see it from where I sat at the foot of the bed.

Langenberg seemed to enjoy Courilof's reaction; he examined his fat, trembling body, turning it over with a smug look on his face that annoyed me.

'It's all right, it's all right.'

'Do I have to stay in bed?'

'Just for a few days . . . not for too long. Do you have a lot to do at the moment?'

'My line of work doesn't allow for breaks,' said Courilof, frowning.

As he was leaving, Langenberg took me aside. 'When you examined him, did you feel a growth?' he said.

I told him I had no doubt about it. He nodded several times. 'Yes, yes.'

'It's cancerous,' I said.

'Well,' he replied, shrugging his shoulders, 'I don't know . . . It's certainly a small tumour, that's for sure . . . If it weren't Courilof, if it were some ordinary person . . . *ein Kerl* . . . I could operate and remove it, which would give him a few more years to live . . . But Courilof! The idea of taking on such responsibility!'

We walked up and down the bright little entrance hall in front of the bedroom.

'Does he know?'

'Of course not,' he replied. 'What good would that do? He's consulted any number of doctors, all of whom suspect the same thing but refuse to operate on him. Courilof!' he repeated. 'You don't understand, my boy, you don't know this country!'

He prescribed a diet and some treatments and left.

The attack lasted about ten days, and I slept in a room adjoining Courilof's, so I could hear him if he called for me. This part of the house was constantly full of the minister's staff, secretaries who brought him files and letters. I watched them wait their turn, shudder and walk over to the closed door; I could hear as they questioned each other in hushed voices: 'What kind of a mood is he in today?'

One of them, a low-ranking staff member whose duties required him to see the minister several times a day, surreptitiously crossed himself when he went into the bedroom. He was rather old, as I recall, dignified and well groomed, with a pale face, tense with anxiety. Courilof, however, almost always spoke in the same tone of voice, measured and polite, cold and curt, hardly moving his lips. He was rarely impatient, but when he was, his voice was barely recognisable from where I waited in the next room. He would hurl abuse in a harsh, breathless voice, then stop suddenly, sigh and wave them away, exclaiming: 'Get out! Go to hell!'

One day, I was standing in the doorway when Madame Courilof noticed a female visitor I'd seen on several occasions. She had one of those pale, ordinary faces that are attractive and hold your attention because of certain clearcut features; her deep-set eyes had a tragic look about them. She stood as straight as a steel beam, and her hair had white streaks in it and rippled over her forehead; she had large teeth, wore a grey cloth dress with a stiff triple collar decorated with lace, all of which gave her a strange and striking appearance. I didn't know her name, but I'd seen her treated with the utmost respect.

When she saw her, Madame Courilof seemed extraordinarily upset; she hesitated for a moment, then made a deep curtsey. The woman looked at her, studying first her golden hair, then her powdered cheeks, then her mouth. She sighed softly, then raised her eyebrows, shaping her pale lips into a sarcastic little smile.

'Is His Excellency feeling better?' she finally murmured angrily.

'My husband is feeling better, yes, Your Highness,' Madame Courilof replied.

There was a brief silence, and the visitor went into the bedroom. Madame Courilof stood in the middle of the room for a moment, not knowing what to do, then slowly walked away. As she passed by me, she smiled sadly, shrugged her shoulders and whispered, 'How oddly these women dress, don't you think?'

When I looked at her closely, I noticed that she looked exhausted and tears had welled up in her eyes.

On another occasion, I met an elderly man in the minister's bedroom who was wearing a white summer uniform. I subsequently learned that it was Prince Nelrode. When Courilof spoke to the prince, his voice changed, becoming as deep and soft as velvet.

When I went in, I saw Courilof half sitting in bed; he'd raised himself up with difficulty, so his features looked strained and pale, but he smiled while nodding his head seriously, with a sort of respectful affection. As soon as he noticed me, his expression changed; he let his head fall grandly back on to the pillow and said under his breath: 'In just a moment, Monsieur Legrand, just a moment . . .'

I showed him the injection I had prepared.

The visitor gestured. 'I'll leave you now, my dear friend.'

He looked at me with curiosity, raising his pince-nez to his eyes, then letting them drop down again.

'Yes, Langenberg told me you had a new doctor.'

'A very skilful one,' Courilof said graciously. But then immediately, he gave me a haughty, weary look. 'Off you go, Monsieur Legrand, I'll call for you.'

I was becoming familiar with how Courilof behaved, with his inferiors, his peers, with people he respected or needed. And all his little gestures, his expressions, the words he used, they were all classic, predictable to a certain extent. But every evening when I went into his room and found him alone with his wife, I realised how human nature is truly bizarre.

At night, I would sleep in the same room as he, stretched out on a chaise-longue next to the alcove. I would go up to bed late. The house was usually filled with the sound of footsteps, voices – but hushed, muted, out of a sense of deferential fear, but still audible, like the humming of a beehive. In the evening, everything was silent. It was cold, as it often is in St Petersburg at the end of spring, when the icy winds run down from the north along the Neva River. I remember going into the bedroom where all you could hear was the crackling and spitting of logs in the wood-burning stove. A pink lamp burned in the corner of the room. Next to the bed, sitting on a small, low armchair, Madame Courilof held her husband's hands. When she saw me, she exclaimed in her shrill little birdlike voice: 'Eleven o'clock already? Time for you to get some rest, my darling.'

I would sit down with a book by the window. Within a few minutes, they would forget I was there and quietly continue their conversation.

Gradually I would look up and, in the darkened room, study their faces. They seemed different. He would listen to her endlessly, pressing her hand against his forehead, a faint smile hovering at the corner of his lips (those stony lips that hardly seemed designed to smile). Sometimes even I enjoyed listening to her. Not that she was intelligent, far from it, but she had a way of rambling on that was fascinating, almost as if she couldn't stop herself; it was as relaxing as the steady sound of a brook, or a bird singing. However, she knew when to be silent, how to be still, how to anticipate his every desire, like an old, wise pussycat. Beneath the pinkish light, half hidden in shadow, what stood out were her beautiful eyes and golden hair, its colour fading. Every so often she would give a little cry, shrug her shoulders with the inimitable sound of a woman who has seen all there is to see of life. Sometimes she would let out a kind of involuntary sigh, a cry of: 'Oh! My God, the things I've seen!' and then she would gently stroke Courilof's hand.

'My darling, my poor darling . . .'

For they would forget I was there and would speak to each other endearingly; she would call him 'my sweetheart . . . my love . . . my darling . . .' Such words spoken to Courilof, to the 'ferocious, voracious Killer Whale', moved me.

'Oh!' she said one day. 'Do you think I don't know? I never should have listened to you. What was the point of getting married? We were happy as we were.'

Suddenly, she fell silent: she had undoubtedly remembered I was there. But I sat totally still.

She sighed. 'Valia, do you remember?' she said softly. 'Do you remember how it used to be?'

'Yes,' he replied curtly.

She hesitated, then whispered with a note of fear and hope in her voice, 'What if they get their way . . . Who knows? If you weren't a minister any more, we could leave the country, we could go and live in France, the two of us.'

When she said that, I saw Courilof's face change, tense up. Something harsh and inhuman came over his features, a look in his eyes.

'Ah!' he said, his voice pompous and solemn, gradually growing louder as he spoke. 'Do you actually think I want to stay in power? It's a burden. But as long as the Emperor needs me, I will carry out my duties to the end.'

She bowed her head sadly. He was starting to get restless, tossing and turning in the bed.

'I'll leave you alone,' she murmured.

He hesitated, then opened his eyes and looked at her. 'Sing me a little song before you go, anything . . .' he asked sweetly.

She sang French love songs, old arias from operettas, swinging her legs, swaying her body, moving her head as if she were in the spotlight, undoubtedly as she had been in the past, in the little cabarets in the Iles. And yet, her voice was still beautiful. I turned away so I couldn't see her, so I could just hear her sweet, sonorous song. Looking at her was horrible; she made me feel pity and scorn. But how did *he* feel when he looked at her? I wondered if she had really once been so beautiful that . . . There wasn't a single picture of her in the house.

He watched her without moving, lost in some vague, passionate dream. 'Ah! No one sings like that any more!'

I remember he took her hands, almost stroking them, with an affectionate kind of indifference, as if they were the hands of a friend, a child, a wife of many years. But his eyes were closed, and, little by little, memories from the past surely came back to him. I could see him press her hands more tightly, forcing the blood to rush away from her fingers. She smiled, a bitter, melancholy little grimace on her face.

'The good times are all in the past, my darling.'

He sighed. 'Life passes quickly,' he said, sounding troubled and anxious.

'It's slow enough now. It's youth that goes so quickly.' She whispered a few words to him that I couldn't make out, then shrugged her shoulders. 'Really?' she said.

Her words and gesture must have surely had some

61

special meaning for them both in the past, for she started to laugh, but sadly, as if she were implying *Do you remember? I was young then . . .*

And he imitated her tone of voice and said again: 'Really? What was that? Really? My darling little one.'

When he laughed, his chin trembled and the expression in his eyes became clear and soft.

Then Courilof's children came in: Ina and the boy, Ivan, who was fat and weak, just like Courilof, with pale cheeks, big ears, easily short of breath.

Courilof spoke to the boy with deep affection. He hugged him, stroked him, held him to him for a long time while sighing, 'Ah! This is my son, my heir.' He gently stroked his hair, his arms.

'Look, Monsieur Legrand, he's anaemic,' he added.

And I still remember how he would lower the boy's pale lips and eyelids for me to see.

The girl said nothing, her face was cold and impassive. Nevertheless, she looked like Courilof; she had his mannerisms and voice. She constantly fiddled with a gold necklace she was wearing. Courilof displayed such coldness towards her that he was virtually hostile. He hissed at her when he spoke, looked at her with an expression of annoyance and anger.

The children kissed his hand. He made the sign of the cross on their bowed heads, as well as on the powdered face of his ageing mistress.

Finally, all three of them left.

11

Courilof and his wife were in the habit of writing to each other from their bedrooms; the servants would carry books or fruit from one end of the house to the other until very late at night, with little notes written in pencil.

I sometimes read them out to him, at his request, for he was proud of his wife; he enjoyed having me see her handwriting and style. She wrote in a rambling fashion, teasing and melancholy, that was actually similar to the way she spoke and was quite charming. She often reminded him to ask me about his medicines, treatments or diet, along with endearments like:

'Good night, my one and only darling! Your old, devoted Marguerite.'

Or: 'I cannot wait until tomorrow: a new day is always precious at our age, and tomorrow means I will be able to see you again.'

Once, I read: 'My darling, would you please see an elderly woman, for my sake. She's the widow Aarontchik, who has come a long way from the provinces to seek justice from you. In the past, and long before I had the joy of knowing you, this woman was my lodger in Lodz, and she looked after me devotedly when . . .'

Then followed a series of initials that I read out to Courilof, without understanding what they meant. He frowned and his face took on that sad, sour look I was beginning to know so well.

He let out a deep sigh. 'File it.'

That same night he thought for a moment, then asked me, 'Don't you find that French women have an innately graceful and elegant sense of style?'

He didn't wait for my reply but continued, 'Ah! If only you could have seen Marguerite Eduardovna in *La Périchole*, when I first met her!'

'Was that a long time ago?' I asked.

He always seemed upset and surprised when I asked him a question, like someone who blushes in embarrassment for a rude person. I recall one day, during the Revolution, when I was interrogating one of the grand dukes. Which one was he? I've forgotten his name, but he was elderly. He'd been in prison in the Kresty jail for more than a year and was dying of hunger when he was brought to me. But he remained cool and calm, treating his guards with meticulous, ironic politeness, seeming to bear his misfortunes with extraordinary stoicism. Right up until the moment when I came into the room. I hadn't slept in thirty-six hours, and I sat down opposite him without the customary formalities. This man, whose face had been half smashed by one of the guards, blushed, not out of anger, but rather out of embarrassment, as if I had taken all my clothes off in front of him. Poor Courilof had also picked up certain mannerisms from Alexander III; he too sometimes looked like a dictator.

I waited while he stared at me for a moment with a haughty, anxious look in his pale, wide eyes.

'It's been fourteen years,' Courilof said at last. He thought for a moment, then added, 'I was young then too . . . A lot of water has gone under the bridge since then.'

At night, as I have already mentioned, I slept in his room. He was patient and never complained. He often couldn't sleep, and I would hear him quietly tossing and turning, moaning as he tried to pick something up from the table.

I remember certain nights in Switzerland, sleepless nights when you listened for every sound, the blood rushing through your veins, the quick pulse at your temples, times when you could smell death oozing from your body, when you were so very weary . . . and at those times, life seemed so wonderful and the nights so long.

'Can't you sleep?' I once asked.

I'd been listening to him for nearly an hour, turning his pillow over and over, no doubt unable to find a cool place on the pillowcase. I knew that feeling very well. He seemed unbelievably happy to hear the sound of my voice. I pulled back the screen that separated the chaise-longue where I slept in the alcove from the rest of the bedroom. He sighed softly.

'Good Lord, I'm in so much pain,' he said, his voice breathless and trembling. 'It feels like a razor's cutting into me.'

'That's usually what it feels like when you have your attacks,' I said. 'It will pass.'

He nodded several times with visible difficulty.

'You're brave,' I said.

I had already noticed that this man had a pathological,

childish need to be praised. He blushed slightly, sat up, leaned against his pillow and pointed to a chair next to his bed where I should sit down.

'I am extremely religious, Monsieur Legrand; I know that young people today lean more towards rationalism. But the courage you are kind enough to recognise in me, and that even my enemies acknowledge as indisputable, comes from my trust in God. Not a single hair falls from anyone's head without his permission.'

He fell silent and we watched the mosquitoes buzzing around, attracted by the light of the lamp. Even now, in summer, whenever I see mosquitoes flying about and twitching their greedy noses, my thoughts return to those nights in the Iles. I can still hear the metallic, lyrical hum of their delicate wings above the water.

I closed the window, saw he was burning up with fever; he didn't seem able to sleep. I offered to read to him. He accepted, thanking me. I took a book down from the shelf. After a few pages, he stopped me.

'Monsieur Legrand, aren't you sleepy? Really?'

I said that I slept badly when the nights were light like this.

'Would you help me?' he said. 'I have a lot of work to catch up on. I'm very worried about it. Don't say anything to Langenberg,' he continued, forcing a smile.

I brought him the stack of letters he pointed out; I passed them to him one at a time, and he scribbled notes in the margins in different coloured pencils that he chose with the utmost care. I furtively glanced at the letters as I handed them to him: they were letters from strangers, for the most part, full of suggestions about suppressing revolutionary ideas in the secondary schools and universities; and an unbelievable number of denunciations, by teachers of students, students of other students. Secondary school students, university students, head teachers, schoolmasters: it seemed as if everyone in Russia spent their lives spying and denouncing each other.

Then came the reports. One of them described serious disruptions in the university in one of the provincial cities (Kharkov, I think); the minister asked me to take down his reply; it was the text of an order he was planning.

He was sitting up against his pillows; the more he dictated, the more severe and cold his face became. He spoke each word individually, with an air of dignity, punctuating them with the same wave of his hand. He ordered them to cancel the lectures. Then he thought for a while, and a grim smile hovered over his lips and in the corners of his half-closed eyes.

'Write this down, Monsieur Legrand: "The time wasted in useless political discussions will be made up during the forthcoming holidays: these will be shortened by the duration of the disruptions. If, in spite of this, the disruptions continue into the autumn, the exam results will be null and void; all the students, whatever their grades may have been, will be required to start their course over again from the beginning."'

Once he'd hissed that out, he looked at me smugly.

'That will make them think twice,' he said, sounding threatening and scornful. 'The next one, please, Monsieur Legrand.'

For this one he dictated a memo intended for schoolteachers:

'During Russian Literature and History lessons, you must take advantage of every opportunity to use the facts in order to awaken in the tender souls of your young students a passionate love for HM the Emperor and the Imperial Family, as well as an indissoluble attachment to the sacred traditions and institutions of the Monarchy. In addition, the words and actions of all the teachers will be designed to be an example of Christian humility and true orthodox charity to your students. It goes without saying that any statements, reading, and, in general, any subversive actions you have the opportunity of noting amongst the students entrusted to your care, must, as always, be punished most severely.'

Next there were requests for appointments. I saw a letter signed by Sarah Aarontchik, begging His Excellency to arrest someone called Mazourtchik, who was guilty of having 'corrupted' her sixteen-year-old son by making him read Karl Marx. Valerian Alexandrovitch, who seemed transformed from the minute he was dealing with his correspondence, made a gesture. His eyes were gleaming behind his glasses; his wide, shiny forehead shone bizarrely, lit up by the lamp.

'Wait a moment. Pass me that note from my wife.'

He re-read it closely, placing it in a coloured folder where various other papers were organised. Then he took out fifteen or so documents and requests for appointments and spread them out on the bed.

'This is the batch for tomorrow and the next day,' he said with pride.

I continued passing him the letters I held in my hand. Finally he stopped me, saying he was tired. He lay there, stretched out, his eyes closed, and sighed. A severe, weary expression came over his face, an expression I knew very well. The night when they had brought the bodies for him to see, in the courtyard of the university, he had had the same nervous tension in his lips, the same rigidity of his features.

'Is it true that the army killed six students last month?' I asked suddenly. 'What did they do?'

He frowned. 'Who told you about that?' he asked quickly, his voice dry and suspicious.

I gave him the vaguest reply I could. He looked straight at me and suddenly spoke most passionately. 'Those poor children . . . just imagine . . . and from good families. They had chased their history professor out of the lecture hall, thrown stones at him! Nothing important.' He sighed sarcastically. 'It was all because of the instigators, professional revolutionaries, a diabolical lot who will end up destroying everything that is good and noble in Russia. I was forced by public outrage and general indignation to clamp down . . . I ordered the leaders arrested and the lecture rooms emptied and called in the troops to evacuate the university. Six of these unfortunate fanatics barricaded themselves up inside the empty classrooms. A shot was fired. By whom? I don't know any more than you do. But a soldier was wounded. In spite of my express orders, the colonel opened fire. Six unfortunate youngsters were killed. Not a single weapon was found on any of them. What can you do! Whose fault was it? The colonel was inconsolable; the soldiers had simply obeyed orders. These youngsters had been rash, presumptuous, I had to clamp down. There are some inexplicable contradictions.

Someone said afterwards: "The shot was fired by an agent provocateur." All this comes under the jurisdiction of my colleague at the Home Office, but he's denying everything and landing me with all the responsibility. But the people who are truly guilty are those vultures, the revolutionaries,' he said, stressing each and every syllable. 'Wherever they go, they bring chaos and death.'

He fell silent. I noticed he'd been mumbling as if he were delirious. I was careful not to interrupt him.

'No one wanted the sinner to die,' he continued, 'but misfortunes happen. Nevertheless, when it is one's duty to lead, one cannot stop at that. *Dura lex, sed lex*: the law is hard, but it is the law. Such things have always happened and will always happen,' he said passionately.

As he talked, I could see his face changing, growing paler, taking on a look of slyness and anguish. I said nothing.

'You see, Monsieur Legrand,' he continued, 'the whole country is defended against revolution by an extremely complex system, a Wall of China made of restrictions, prejudices, superstitions, traditions, you might even call them, but they are extremely sturdy, for the pressure of the enemy is much stronger than you could ever imagine. And at the slightest hint of weakness, the slightest crack, the enemy will make sure that everything comes crashing down. This is what Prince Alexander Alexandrovitch Nelrode, my friend, has said himself, and it is gospel. He is a true statesman, Monsieur Legrand, and a true gentleman.'

He pronounced this word with touching, comical solemnity and the slightly sibilant affected accent of a pure-bred Englishman.

It was nearly morning. I switched off the lamp. He had become greatly agitated as he spoke and was burning with fever; even a few steps away from him, I could feel the heat coming from his body. I changed the hot compresses and gave him something to drink. He was struggling to breathe and the swollen area around his liver was rising and falling like a balloon.

'Why is it,' he asked in a softer, fainter, shaky voice, 'why do I feel such a terrible pain on my right side, as if a crab is digging into my flesh with its claws?'

I said nothing. In any case, he didn't really seem to see me.

'God! I'm not afraid of death!' he said suddenly. 'It is a great joy to die a Christian, with a clear conscience, having served my religion and my Emperor.'

Suddenly his pompous, solemn tone changed once again, became anxious, full of a kind of zeal and goodwill. 'I haven't touched a single penny of the money entrusted to me by the state. I will leave empty-handed, just as I arrived when I came to power.'

He sighed weakly, finally seeming to recognise me. 'Thank you, Monsieur Legrand. Would you be kind enough to give me something to drink?'

I handed him a glass and he drank the cold tea, panting like a dog quenching its thirst. I left him alone and went to lie down. The heat in the room and the stench of fever made me drowsy. I finally fell asleep, feeling I was being tossed from one nightmare to the next.

12

Courilof recovered; at least, Langenberg allowed him to go and present his report to the Emperor, and from that day on, I no longer saw my Killer Whale. Our paths would sometimes cross in the rooms on the lower floor, next to the office. He would nod at me as he passed by, and say in his pompous, mocking voice: 'Are you getting used to the climate of the Palmyra of the North, my dear Monsieur Legrand?'

And, without waiting for my reply, he would nod his wide smooth forehead several times and murmur: 'Yes, yes, of course.' And with an absent-minded, kindly wave of the hand, he would keep going.

Whenever I asked him about his health, he would smile and say, '*Nil desperandum*,' slightly raising his voice, undoubtedly to arouse the admiration of all the scroungers gathered around him. 'I have never had a tendency towards hypochondria, thank God! Work, now that's the true fountain of youth!'

At that time, I became close to Froelich, with the goal of finding out details regarding the minister's first wife. Utterly pointless but I was curious! Froelich had known her well; he had raised the Courilofs' nephew, Hippolyte Nicolaévitch, who, at present, held an important post at the ministry under Courilof. (He was called 'Little Courilof' or 'Courilof the Thief' to distinguish him from his uncle.)

Froelich had been his tutor for fifteen years, right up until the death of the first Madame Courilof. In response to my questions, he hesitated slightly, then said, 'You are familiar with the reputation of Her Majesty the Empress Alexandra? Mysticism bordering on madness. The first wife of His Excellency was the same. By the end of her life, she was completely mad.' He replied touching his finger to his forehead. 'His Excellency's private life has not been easy . . .'

'And now?' I asked.

Froelich gave a little whistle of delight; he had thin, tight lips, an anxious look in his eyes; he rubbed his hands together, glanced nervously around him. 'The beautiful Margot,' he said quickly, 'will ruin His Excellency's career. The only reason he hasn't already fallen out of favour by now is because Prince Nelrode is his friend and has protected him. And, truthfully, isn't it scandalous that the Minister of Education, whose main function is to protect Russian youth from the path of evil, gives them instead, by this marriage, an example of loose morals?'

He fidgeted with his pince-nez for a moment. 'It appears she was once very beautiful,' he observed, with regret.

A few days later, Prince Nelrode came to lunch at the Iles. I recognised the elderly man with the weary, delicate eyes I'd once met in the minister's room when he'd been ill. In 1888, Prince Nelrode had narrowly survived a terrorist attack. His assailant, someone named Grégoire Semenof, aged seventeen, had easily been overcome by the prince's soldiers. And the prince arranged for a rather barbaric, though efficient, execution; his men kicked Semenof in the head until he was dead.

There was another story about Nelrode. During one of the uprisings in Poland, when the town square was covered in dead bodies, he had a thin layer of dirt scattered over them and instructed his squadrons to carry out manoeuvres there, crushing and levelling the earth for six hours, until there remained nothing of these fallen men but a bit of dust.

The other guests were Langenberg, Baron Dahl, his son Anatole and the Minister of Foreign Affairs (one of the three such ministers who had been labelled 'foreign to foreign affairs', a nickname that was an instant success). Unbelievably old and pale, hunched up like a compass and as light as a dead leaf, his head constantly shaking, smelling of violets, he took a quarter of an hour to cross the terrace, leaning on Courilof's arm. In his hazy eyes, he had the dreamy, sad look of a very ancient horse dying of old age in his stable. His conversation, in the purest, most classical French, was so dotted with circumlocutions, euphemisms, allusions to events of a former age long forgotten by everyone, that he seemed unintelligible, not only to me but to his colleagues as well. It was obvious, however, that they happily listened to him, as if he were speaking a classical language that was mysterious and poetic.

I looked at Dahl with curiosity: I knew from Froelich that he was the sworn enemy of Courilof and his eventual successor at the Ministry of Education. He was fat, of average height; his neck was short and thick, his head shaved in the German style. His eyelashes, eyebrows and moustache were a faded blond that blended into his greyish pale face. He had bulging cold eyes, like certain fish, very wide nostrils that breathed in deeply, and a look on his face that was simultaneously arrogant and nervous, the kind of expression you see on certain international criminals. Froelich told me that, in his youth, Dahl had been a notorious pederast (Froelich called it 'dubious morals'), but now Dahl seemed to have settled down, desiring only the pursuit of a brilliant career.

Marguerite Eduardovna sat at the place of honour. Wearing make-up and powder, with pearls around her neck and her body poured into her long, tight corset and lace bodice, she said nothing. She seemed not even to hear the men's conversation, just stared sadly out into space.

Almost immediately, the conversation turned to the Emperor and the imperial family. The expressions they used to discuss them – 'His Majesty deigned to grant me the immense honour of allowing me an audience with him ... When I had the profound pleasure of seeing our beloved sovereign ...' – were spoken with such mockery and scorn that the words took on a tone of intentional farce. Nelrode, in particular, excelled at it. He looked at the gold-framed portrait of the Emperor on the wall opposite him and a smile fluttered across his lips, a spark of intelligence flared in his delicate, weary eyes.

'You all appreciate the goodness, the magnificent soul, the angelic innocence of our dearly beloved sovereign, don't you?' Courilof gave a little ironic sigh and fell silent. The others nodded, and the same amused twinkle lit up their eyes. What he really meant was: 'You all know that Emperor Nicolas is hardly intelligent'; everyone understood what he was saying, and each of them believed himself the only one to understand. Courilof was obviously attempting this sarcastic, nonchalant tone. But he couldn't quite manage it; a hatred he could barely disguise made his voice quiver the moment he said the Emperor's name. Dahl stopped eating and drinking for a moment then, looked at Courilof for a long time, his eyes half closed yet staring at him ironically, as if he were watching Courilof performing on a tight rope.

Sometimes one of the guests would secretly glance over towards the end of the table where Courilof's daughter sat next to Dahl's son, Baron Anatole, a large, pale young man of twenty. His mouth gaped open, his cheeks were puffy, his eyelashes white: the spitting image of the suckling pig you eat at Easter. He listened to no one and spoke in a sharp, monotonous voice that now and again shot through the noise of the conversation like a plane in a tailspin.

'The ball that Princess Barbe gave was all in all more successful, *a grander affair*, than Princess Anastasie's ball . . .'

Dahl and Courilof both frowned and made a point of looking away. A long discussion about censorship followed. It was late, nearly four o'clock, and still no one thought of leaving the table. It was a beautiful, sunny day; the rose-bushes in the gardens swayed in the wind; beyond the treetops, you could see St Petersburg in the distance, like a dark cloud topped in gold.

Censorship of personal correspondence was a tradition

that the elderly Minister of Foreign Affairs deemed appropriate, 'having proved its worth'. But the prince thought it dangerous.

'A statesman should not allow himself to feel personal animosity,' he said, 'and the practice of reading the correspondence of one's enemies can only lead to such feelings. When I read that our dear Ivan Petrovitch refers to me as a blood-thirsty tiger, it makes no difference that I am hardened by fifty years of service to the imperial court of holy Russia, for my sins, it still upsets me. I am only human ... What's the point of knowing too much? It is always better, always wiser, to close one's eyes.'

'Excellent advice for certain husbands,' said the elderly minister.

After he said this, he laughed; his false teeth rattled several times in his empty mouth, and he looked squarely at Marguerite Eduardovna, with the dreamy, sad expression of a melancholy old horse who chews its cud and stares blankly out in space. Courilof took the insult without saying a word, without flinching, but he frowned slightly, and his face appeared paler and harsher.

The conversation continued, turning to the appointment of a new governor general in P ... and he replied to Dahl in a steady voice. It was only several moments later, when no one was looking as Nelrode told some anecdote about a civil servant accused of misappropriation of public funds and theft, that my Courilof sighed softly, cautiously, and let his head drop heavily down.

The prince lifted the glass of wine in front of him to his lips, smelled it without drinking it, as if it were a bouquet of flowers. He put it down again, shrugged his shoulders in his familiar way, and said: 'Who hasn't His Majesty Emperor Nicolas appointed as governor general! *O tempora! O mores!* It's exactly the same with the Saint George Cross. It's handed out like candy these days! Now when His Majesty Alexander III was Emperor . . .'

He stopped for a moment, sighed, thought for a while, then murmured: 'Sad, such a very sad day for Russia when that sovereign died!'

'Definitely,' said Courilof enthusiastically. *'Juvenile consilium, latens odium, privatum odium, haec tria omnia regna perdiderunt.* (Childish advice, envious conspiracy and private hatred have brought down kingdoms.) Nevertheless, no one reveres and, dare I say, adores His Majesty Emperor Nicolas more than I do, but it is unfortunately true that a certain softness, a certain nobility of character, doesn't quite fit with exercising absolute power.'

'But it is very kind to be noble and sensitive, like His Majesty,' said the prince, slightly sneering, his tone unmistakably filled with respectful scorn. 'That is how he recently granted Emperor William a commercial treaty that is very advantageous to Germany but infinitely less so for Russia . . . His Majesty, our dearly beloved Emperor Nicolas, couldn't refuse Emperor William anything; he was the Emperor's guest at the time, as he did me the honour of telling me himself.'

'Tamen, semper talis . . . Still, and always, the same,' murmured Courilof.

'I have noticed throughout my very long life,' the elderly Minister of Foreign Affairs said slowly, 'that princes are too inclined to follow the noble instincts of their magnanimous hearts. It falls to their ministers to balance such tendencies with practical realities and economic necessity.'

He smiled and suddenly seemed to me infinitely less stupid and inoffensive than I'd thought; a gleam suddenly illuminated his lifeless eyes. At that very moment, he looked at me. I was bathed in sunlight; this was the reason, without a doubt, why my face stood out in the dimness and caught his near-blind glance from amongst everyone else. He nodded towards me.

'Monsieur is getting an education,' he said in a voice that was kindly, mocking and scornful all at once, the same tone my Courilof tried to imitate without managing it.

Marguerite Eduardovna saw her husband give her a look and stood up to leave; I was about to go with her when Courilof called me back. 'Stay. The prince would like you to recommend something for his asthma.'

I sat down again and, after some time, they forgot about me. I'd stopped listening to them. I was bored and tired. They were smoking and speaking more loudly. I heard Dahl's sudden laughter, the Killer Whale's voice, and the prince. I remember thinking about Fanny, about the Party leaders in Geneva. I looked at the sun over the grounds and started to automatically recite the months . . . July, August, September . . . 'Ceremonies and public holidays don't really start until the autumn . . .' I felt a vague sense of sadness. At that very moment, I was struck by Nelrode's voice (they were going on about the run-up to the Russo-Japanese War):

'No one wants war. Not the sovereign, not the ministers. In fact, no one ever wants war or any other sort of crime, but that doesn't stop it. Because the people in power are weak human beings, not blood-thirsty monsters, as everyone imagines them to be. *Lord*, wouldn't that be preferable!'

He took the elderly Minister for Foreign Affairs by the arm. 'It just makes my blood boil! These children, these incompetents . . . Still! All that will pass very quickly! As we will . . . So what?' he said. He shrugged his shoulders wearily, closed his eyes and began reciting:

'*So what if your life went entirely according to your wishes?*

'*So what if you'd read the Book of Life straight to the end?*

'Good Lord! What are we doing in this hell? We're not greedy animals, yet we're wasting our lives in vain pursuits, seeking favour and friendship from the sovereign.'

'You are still young,' said the elderly minister bitterly. 'Wait until you have reached the very end of your days, as I have, and see the coldness and hostility of the princes replace the trust and goodwill they have bestowed upon you before! . . . Do you know that since last Christmas, I've been prevented from having private meals with the sovereigns? I feel,' he suddenly exclaimed with extraordinary vehemence, a despairing tone of the betrayed lover in his voice that made me smile, 'I truly feel that you can't recover the past! I cannot sacrifice the little time I have left to these ungrateful rulers. It's killing me, I say it openly, it's slowly killing me!'

He stopped, and I thought I saw tears glistening in his eyes. I turned around to look at him more closely. I was right; from his cloudy eyes, the vacant eyes of a very old animal, a single tear-drop fell. I felt a mixture of scorn and pity.

Courilof, however, had taken some pornographic Japanese prints out of a locked cabinet, and they were all leaning towards him, laughing nervously, their hands shaking. A long time afterwards, they started talking about women. I watched Courilof. He was a different man, his eyes sparkling, his voice husky, his fingers trembling.

'There's a new singer,' said the prince, 'at the Villa Rodé, a fifteen-year-old girl, still thin and plain, but with the most beautiful hair in the world, and her voice. Pieces of gold thrown against a crystal platter wouldn't make such a pure, brilliant sound.'

'Villa Rodé,' said Dahl.

He deliberately stopped himself, looked at Courilof, his eyes half closed.

'No one really knows how to sing any more, now that Marguerite Eduardovna has left!' said Dahl.

Courilof frowned and suddenly the excitement was gone from his face; he went pale, became anxious and sombre once more.

'Well, gentlemen,' he said, 'let's go out into the garden, shall we.'

13

On the terrace, I could hear Langenberg finishing a conversation he'd started with Dahl. 'We should create a secret society with the purpose of exterminating all these damned socialists, revolutionaries, communists, free thinkers, and all the Jews, of course. We could recruit former thieves, common criminals, in exchange for sparing their lives. These revolutionary thugs deserve no more pity than mad dogs,' he said.

Courilof and the prince had stopped and were smiling as they listened to him talk.

'Damn it! My boy,' said the prince, 'how you do go on. But we're far from that point, unfortunately!'

They went down into the garden. Dahl, Langenberg and the elderly Minister of Foreign Affairs soon left. Courilof and the prince were alone.

'How can you and I prevent ourselves from leaning towards the liberalism we're reproached for at court?' I heard Courilof say. 'When one hears such stupidity, it's heart-breaking.'

The elderly prince stopped. He'd asked permission to put on his cap, for it was very hot for the season. He was standing in the middle of the path lined with white roses. I was walking behind them, but they took no notice of me. He carefully put on an English cap that had a large peak lined in green silk, pulled it down over his eyes, and said, in French, his voice deep and weary, 'Sticks and stones.' He struck the ground sharply with his cane.

'I will never regret having been humane,' he said. 'At my age especially, Valerian Alexandrovitch, you'll see, it is a great consolation.'

He had long, pale hands; I can still picture them. I vividly imagined that morning in Poland when he'd launched the squadron into the little town square covered in blood and dead bodies.

At the time, I listened to him with ironic disbelief. Later on, when I had taken their place, I understood there had not been an ounce of hypocrisy in what these men said. They simply had a short memory, as we all do.

They talked about the assassination attempts of the revolutionaries. They were sitting on a bench, at a place called the Rond Pont des Muses. I can still picture the yew trees trimmed into bizarre shapes, and the scent of the box trees. I had slipped behind the hedge. I was so close that I could have stretched out my hand and touched them. I listened to them speak with passionate curiosity.

'I'm often warned,' said the prince, 'that assassinations are being planned, and people write to me or have me told: "Don't go here, or there." I never listen to them. But I have to admit, when I'm at home at night, going to bed, knowing that the next day I have to go somewhere, I'm frightened. But as soon as I get into my car, it's all right.'

'Well,' said Courilof, 'I say my prayers every morning

when I wake up. I take each new day as the last day of my life. When I get home in the evening, I thank God for having granted me one more day.'

He fell silent. He had spoken in the tone of banal solemnity that I knew so well, but his voice was shaking.

'Ah! Yes,' said the prince, in his inimitable way, 'you believe in God . . .' He let out a weary little laugh. 'Well, as for me,' he murmured, 'I do my best to believe, but I swear I don't know why. I get a certain personal satisfaction out of it, not a feeling of contentment at having fulfilled my obligations, Valerian Alexandrovitch, but the bitter satisfaction of seeing, once again, how very stupid people are. As for posterity and all that nonsense, I'm not interested. Think of how much noise they made over what happened to that anarchist Semenof! I spared him months of suffering, you know, the anguish and fear of being executed, and, at the same time, avoided a trial that would only have encouraged ideas in people we'd then have to fight. It was the same in Poland. Having the horses trample dead bodies couldn't do them any more harm, you have to admit that, and inspiring terror did them good; it stopped the insurrection dead and so saved human lives. The more I see, the more value I place on human life . . . and less on what they like to call "ideas",' he continued as if in a dream. 'In a word, I behaved rationally. And that is what people cannot forgive.'

'Well I have faith in posterity,' murmured Courilof. 'Russia will forget my enemies, but she will not forget me. It's all very hard, very difficult,' he kept saying with a sigh. 'They say you have to be capable of shedding blood, and it's true.'

He stopped for a moment, then added quietly: 'For a just cause.'

'I don't believe in just causes much either,' sighed the prince. 'But I'm a good deal older than you, it's true; you still have illusions.'

'It's hard; life is difficult,' the minister said again, sadly. He fell silent for a moment, then said quietly: 'I have so many problems.'

I leaned forward even more. This was my first really dangerous move since I'd been in the minister's house. But I was gripped by intense curiosity.

The prince gave a little cough, then turned and looked at Courilof. I could see the two of them, a few metres from me, through the break in the hedge. I held my breath.

Courilof began complaining: he was overworked, ill, surrounded by enemies who plotted against him.

'Why didn't I listen to you? Why did I get married?' he said over and over again, bitterly. 'A statesman must be invulnerable. *They* know,' he said, strongly stressing each word. '*They* know where it hurts the most, and every time I get ahead, that's where *they* strike. My life has become a living hell. If you only knew what filth, what crass lies are told every day about my wife!'

'I know, my poor friend, I know,' the prince said softly.

'For Ina's twentieth birthday,' Courilof continued, 'I was planning to give a ball, as is our tradition. You know that Their Majesties have never set foot in my house since the day my wife died. Well, just imagine,' he exclaimed, his voice shaking, 'that our sovereigns let it be known to me that if they were to attend the ball, it would be better if Marguerite Eduardovna were not there! And I was forced to smile, to take the insult in silence. It is inconceivable that a man in my position, who strikes fear into the hearts of thousands of people, should be forced to bow before this crowd, this mass of lazy louts who make up the court. Ah! I'm tired of being in power! But I am fulfilling my obligation by remaining.' He said this several times, passionately.

'It is true that if Marguerite Eduardovna could leave Russia for a while . . .' the prince began.

'No,' said Courilof. 'Personally, I would rather end it once and for all and leave as well. She is my wife before God. She bears my name. And anyway, why should they drag up the past? Do they even know what happened then? When they called her a "loose woman", they said it all. I'm not talking about love; I'm not talking about the early years; but as for the devotion she has shown me, the comfort, the help she has been to me for fourteen years, only I can be the judge of that. My life! My miserable life! My poor first wife, you know the lengths I went to care for her; no one, not even you, can know how much I have . . .'

He wanted to say 'suffered', but the word refused to cross his proud lips. He stood up taller, making a weary gesture with his hand. 'She's dead. Her poor soul is with God! But didn't *I* have the right to rebuild my life as I saw fit? I can see now that the private life of a statesman belongs to the public, like his work. As soon as you try to keep a little piece of your life for yourself, that's exactly where your enemies strike.'

'Margot,' the elderly prince said, as if in a dream. 'Even today, though she's older, less beautiful, she still has an inexplicable charm. Without a doubt, the same kind of charm we find in people whom we have greatly loved.'

'As for me,' said Courilof, sounding so sincere that I was struck by it, 'I loved her long ago; you know how many mad things I did for her, but none of that compares with how I feel about her now. I am alone in life, Alexander Alexandrovitch, we are all alone. The higher our positions, the more complete our solitude. In her, God has given me a friend. I have many faults – man is but a mass of faults and misery – but I am loyal. I do not abandon my friends.'

'Be careful of Dahl,' said the prince. 'He wants your post, and in my opinion, they are only waiting for you to make a false move to give it to him. And Dahl was a former colleague of yours at the ministry. Who else would set us up if not our colleagues? Why don't you marry off your daughter to his imbecile of a son? A rich dowry would appease him. He only wants power for the money it will bring.'

Courilof hesitated. 'Ina is disgusted by the very idea of such a marriage,' he said. 'And in any case, I'm afraid it wouldn't solve anything. Dahl is one of those insatiable dogs who not only eats the meat off the bone, but the bone as well.'

'You've heard, haven't you,' asked the prince, 'about his latest masterpiece? You know that the pet subject at court for some time now is *Russia for the Russians*. In order to get a contract for the railways, for example, you have to have a name that ends in *of*. The baron dug up a poor little penniless prince from somewhere or other who has a traditional name. He's using it to get contracts for mines or railways that he then sells on to Jews or Germans, after taking a fair commission for himself. Two thousand roubles for the prince, and presto! Amusing, don't you think?'

'Every now and again I am staggered by the extraordinary greed of these people,' said Courilof. 'An ordinary man has the right to be greedy, because he knows that otherwise he would starve to death. But these people who have everything – money, friends in high places, property – they never have enough! I just don't understand it.'

'Each of us has his weaknesses. Human nature is incomprehensible. One cannot even say with certainty whether a man is good or evil, stupid or intelligent. There does not exist a good man who has not at some time in his life committed a cruel act, nor an evil man who has not done good, nor an intelligent man who has never been foolish, nor a fool who has never acted intelligently! Still, that's what gives life its diversity, its surprises. I find that idea rather amusing.'

They had stood up as they talked and walked away from the Rond Pont. I waited for a while and then left as well.

14

They stayed in the garden for the rest of the day, along with Ivan, Courilof's son, who listened to them, looking bored.

'For him,' said the minister, 'life will be better.'

I could hear everything they said; their words carried through the calm summer air.

'We're going through difficult times, but if public opinion were only on our side, I am convinced that we would get back on our feet.'

'As for me,' said Courilof, 'you could never know how much it comforts me when people are sympathetic towards me. Society is weary of flirting with the idea of a revolution. I think we have ten or twelve hard years ahead. But the future is marvellous.'

'My dear boy . . .' the prince murmured, sounding sceptical. But he said no more.

Courilof, lost in thought, caressed his son's hair. The boy yawned furtively, nervously, but he couldn't stop his entire body from trembling, a sign of the instinctive repugnance that children feel when touched by elderly hands.

I imagined Courilof's secret thoughts very well. 'Her

Imperial Highness seems distressed by the birth of Grand Duchess Anastasia,' he said, as if speaking them out loud. 'This fourth disappointment is difficult. Their Majesties are still young, it's true . . .'

There was a long silence. Then the prince shook the ash off his cigarette.

'Yesterday I saw His Royal Highness the Grand Duke Michael,' he said, pouting. 'He really is the spitting image of his noble father.'

Both of them were now looking at the little boy and smiling, as if, through him, they could see the shape of the future: the Emperor dying without an heir; his brother, the Grand Duke Michael, succeeding him on the throne, an era of peace and happiness for Russia. At least, that's what I was sure Courilof was thinking. The prince's thoughts were more difficult to work out . . . Yes, I remember that day very well indeed.

Finally the prince remembered me and called me over to ask for a remedy for his painful chronic cough. I pointed to his cigarette and told him he should stop smoking.

He began to laugh.

'Youth always goes to extremes. You can take away a man's life, but not his passions.'

He had a precise way of speaking and a brilliantly dry way of expressing himself. I suggested he take a sedative. He agreed, thanking me. I left. I remained in my room for a long time, musing and wondering whose dreams and speculations about the future, ours or theirs, were fair. I was extremely sad and tired, but filled with feelings of blissful savagery, feelings that surprised even me.

When I returned to the garden, it was late and dusk

was falling, the sort of dusk you get in springtime. The sky was clear and brilliant, like deep, transparent rose crystal. At moments like these, the Iles were truly beautiful. The little lagoons formed by the water, between two strips of land, shimmered faintly and reflected the sky.

The prince's carriage had pulled up; he was sitting in the back with a fur blanket over his legs. He held some fresh white roses, cut especially for him, and was stroking them.

I gave him the prescription for the sedative.

'Are you French, Monsieur?' he asked me.

'Swiss.'

He nodded.

'A beautiful country ... I'm going to spend a month in Vevey this summer.'

He signalled the driver with a little kick, and the door closed. The carriage set off.

On the road back to St Petersburg, near the city gates, a woman – the former fiancée of Grégoire Semenof, who had been waiting for this moment for fifteen years – threw a bomb into the prince's carriage. They were all blown to bits: the horses, the driver, the elderly man who was peacefully smelling his roses, along with the assassin herself.

15

Courilof learned of the assassination that same evening. We were at dinner. One of the officers in the prince's entourage came in. As soon as Courilof heard the sound of the sabre striking the paving stones, he seemed to guess something terrible had happened. He jumped in fright, so suddenly that he dropped the glass of wine he was holding; it crashed against the leg of the table. But almost immediately, he regained control of himself, stood up and went out without saying a word. Marguerite Eduardovna followed him.

That night I could clearly see his window from my room. His lights were on, and I watched him pace slowly back and forth until morning. I saw his shadow go over to the windows, peer out, turn slowly around, disappear into the other side of the room, then come back into view.

The next day, when he saw me, he just murmured weakly, 'Have you heard . . .'

'Yes.'

He brought his hand to his head, looking at me with his wide, pale eyes.

'I knew him for thirty years,' he finally said.

That was all. Then he quickly turned away and made a weary gesture.

'Well, there you have it . . . It's over.'

The next day I received a message from Fanny, which both surprised and worried me, for she was not supposed to take such risks, and it had been agreed she would contact me only to set the date for Courilof's assassination.

She asked me to meet her in Pavlovsk, about an hour outside St Petersburg, in front of the Kursaal Concert Hall.

There was a piano and violin recital in Pavlovsk. We met in the entrance, where a great crowd of people were silently listening to music by Schumann. I can still remember those bright, rapid chords.

Fanny had once again disguised herself as a kind of peasant. I told her rather angrily that we were involved in a game that was theatrical and distasteful enough without making it even more complicated and dangerous with elaborate costumes. Afterwards, in fact, my long experience as a revolutionary taught me that nothing is more likely to destroy a mission than excessive precautions. Beneath her red head-scarf, her long Jewish nose and thick lips would have betrayed her more surely than her real passport. But there was a large crowd; no one saw her, or they thought she was a servant.

We went out into the grounds, where the mist, at dusk, was as thick as a cloud. We sat down on a bench. The fog surrounded us like a dense wall: two steps away, a yew tree was half hidden by a damp, thick, white haze, like the milky sap that comes out of certain types of plants when you cut their stems. Even the air had the sweet scent of foliage, a sickly smell that irritated my throat.

I was coughing. Fanny, annoyed, removed the red scarf from her head.

'Bad news, comrade. Lydie Frankel, who was keeping the dynamite in her house, was killed in an explosion. In Geneva, they decided to hand over that part of the mission to me. I'll get hold of the bombs when we need them. The assassination will probably be set for autumn. I have some letters for you from Switzerland.'

I took the letters, automatically putting them into my pocket.

Fanny laughed nervously. 'Are you really going to keep those letters in your overcoat so they can fall into the hands of the informers? Read them, then burn them.'

I read them; they contained nothing of consequence. Nevertheless, I set fire to them with my cigarette and scattered the ashes about. Fanny leaned towards me.

'Is it true,' she asked eagerly, 'is it true, comrade, that you saw Prince Nelrode a few hours before he died?'

'It's true.'

She questioned me in a low, muffled voice. A savage, doleful flame lit up her green eyes. I said I'd heard the prince and the minister talking to each other.

She listened to me in silence, but I could see what she was thinking in her eyes. She had come closer and was staring at me.

'What?' she finally said.

She stopped; she seemed unable to find words to express her horror.

'What did they say?'

She drew back nervously. By then, the fog had become so dense that Fanny's face was half hidden in the mist. I could hear her voice quivering with passion and hatred. As for me, I was tired and annoyed. She pressed me to answer her questions. I angrily told her that in my opinion, they had said a few reasonable things but also talked a lot of nonsense. Yet I could see it was useless to explain to her how these two politicians, who were feared and hated, with their faults, their insensitivity and their dreams, had seemed as imperfect and unhappy as anyone, including me. She would have read an obscure, secret meaning into my words that they didn't contain.

Meanwhile, the music had stopped; the crowd came out of the concert hall and slowly dispersed along the paths through the grounds. We went our separate ways.

16

It just so happened that the day the widow Aarontchik – the elderly Jewess recommended by Marguerite Eduardovna – came to visit, I was in Courilof's room. He wasn't feeling well; his wife asked me to firmly cut the interview short if I thought he was getting weak or tired. Four days had passed since the assassination. No business had been carried out since then. Courilof spent half of each day at the prince's residence, beside the coffin that contained his mangled remains, with priests who recited prayers imploring peace for the dead man's soul; the rest of the time, Courilof went to church.

Finally, on the fifth day, the funeral took place.

Several supposed accomplices of the female assassin had been arrested. Courilof wanted to be present when these 'monsters, these wolves in sheep's clothing', as he called them, were all interrogated. Afterwards, two of them were hanged.

Courilof came home exhausted; he said nothing, except when he was shouting at the servants or employees at the ministry. Only with me did he remain patient and courteous. He seemed to actually feel a kind of sympathy towards me.

The audience granted to the widow Aarontchik had been delayed like all the others. Courilof received her in an enormous room I'd never been in before, full of portraits of the Emperor and mementoes of Pobiedonostsef and Alexander III, all in glass frames and labelled like jars in a pharmacy. A dazzling light came in through the half-closed, enormous scarlet curtains; they looked stained with fresh blood. He made a savage picture that was striking to behold: his pale, motionless face above the white linen jacket of his uniform, decorations around its collar, others pinned at the side; his hand rested on the table with its heavy gold wedding band, adorned with a red stone that caught the light.

A small, thin woman was shown in; she was shaking. She had white hair, a bony, angular face, a nose like a beak. She was dressed in mourning clothes that looked tarnished in the sunlight. She took three steps forward, then stopped, dumbstruck.

The minister spoke to her in a deep, low, quiet voice, the one he sometimes used with inferiors who'd been recommended to him.

'You are the widow Sarah Aarontchik,' he asked, 'of the Jewish faith?'

'Yes,' she whispered.

Her hands were visibly shaking; she clasped them in front of her and stood motionless.

'Come closer.'

She didn't seem to understand; she looked up at him, blinking, her eyes full of resignation and a kind of holy terror.

His eyes were lowered, his head thrown back; he was

absent-mindedly tapping an open letter on the table, waiting for her to speak.

She remained silent.

'Come now, Madame,' he called out. 'You did ask for an audience, didn't you? You wanted to speak to me. What did you want to say?'

'Your Excellency,' she murmured, 'I met your wife, Marguerite Eduardovna . . .'

'Yes, yes,' he interrupted curtly. 'That has nothing to do with the business that brings you here, I presume?'

'No,' she stammered.

'Well then, get to the point, Madame. My time is precious.'

'The Jacques Aarontchik case, Your Excellency.'

He gestured that he knew all about it.

As she said no more, he sighed, picked up a file, leafed through it for a moment and quickly read out loud: ' "I, the undersigned . . . denounce Pierre Mazourtchik, junior supervisor . . . Hmm! . . . Hmm! . . . Guilty of having corrupted my son . . ." '

He smiled faintly, took another statement from the table and read out loud:

' "I, the undersigned, Vladimirenko, teacher in the secondary school at . . . denounce one Jacques Aarontchik, of Jewish faith, aged sixteen, guilty of having incited revolution and subversive acts in his classmates." Do you accept these facts as true?'

'Your Excellency, my unfortunate child was the victim of an agent provocateur. I thought I had done the right thing, I denounced his tutor, Mazourtchik, who was making him read these books and things . . . I'm just a widow, a poor woman. I didn't know, I couldn't know . . .'

'No one is reproaching you for anything,' said Courilof; his icy, haughty tone stopped the woman dead. 'What is it that you want?'

'I didn't know I was dealing with one of Your Excellency's agents. He also denounced my son. I am just a poor widow.'

I looked at her hands clasped in front of her; they were dirty, with furrows as deep as wounds. It made a horrible impression, and I saw that Courilof was also looking at them, shuddering, but somewhat fascinated. Her hands weren't marked by some rare disease, but by doing the washing, the housework, by boiling water, by old age.

The minister frowned, and I watched his heavy, impatient hands pushing the files about on the table.

'Your son has been expelled,' he said at last. 'I will look into the matter to see if there is reason to believe in his sincere repentance, and I will authorise him to continue his studies, if he proves himself worthy. Up until now, he was the best student at the school, as I can see from his reports, and given his young age . . . In any case, you have made this great journey, despite being elderly and all alone; if you will be responsible for your son, for his political opinions . . .' he said, his voice becoming more and more dry and nervous.

She said nothing. He nodded, indicating that the audience was over.

Then, for the first time, she looked at him.

'Your Excellency, excuse me, but he's dead now.'

'Who's dead?' asked Courilof.

'He is . . . my little . . . Jacques . . .'

'What? Your son?'

'He killed himself, two months ago, Your Excellency, out of de . . . despair,' she mumbled.

And suddenly, she began to cry. She cried in a humble, vile way, with a snorting sound that made you feel sick. Her tiny face, dark red, was suddenly covered in tears; her shrivelled, trembling mouth was wet, gaping, hanging open on one side from the violence of her sobbing.

The more she cried, the more Courilof's face grew heavier, paler.

'When did he die?' he finally asked in his harsh, ringing voice, even though the woman had already told him; but he seemed confused. He spoke automatically, rapidly.

'Two months ago,' she said again.

'Well then, why have you come to see me?'

'To ask for help. He was going to help me, he was about to finish school. He was already earning fifteen roubles a month. Now, I'm all alone. I still have three young children to raise, Your Excellency. Jacques killed himself because he was expelled from school over a mistake. I've brought a letter with me from the head teacher, saying it was clearly a mistake, that the papers and books taken from my son's room had been planted there by Mazourtchik . . . by Your Excellency's agent, because we couldn't pay him the hundred roubles he was demanding. I have all the facts here, the dates, the confession of the guilty party.'

She offered the papers to the minister, who held them in two fingers as if they were rags, then threw them down on the table without even looking at them.

'If I have understood correctly, you are accusing me of your son's death.'

'Your Excellency, I'm just asking for help. He was only sixteen. You are a father, Your Excellency.'

She was shaking and panting so violently that she could barely get the words out of her mouth.

'But why the hell have you come to me?' he suddenly shouted. 'Because of your son? Is there anything I can do about your son? He's dead, God has his soul! There you have it. Get out of here, you have no right coming here and bothering me with your sad story, do you understand?' he thundered. 'Get out of here!'

He was shouting, beside himself, his eyes filled with a kind of terror; he struck everything on the table so hard that the letters fell to the floor.

The elderly Jewess turned very pale. She started to move, then suddenly, we heard her humble, persistent voice once again: 'Just a little help, Your Excellency; you're a father . . .'

I looked at Courilof and saw him wave her away. 'Go,' he said. 'Leave your address at the ministry. I'll send you some money.'

Suddenly he threw his head back against the chair and started to laugh. 'Go!'

She left. He continued laughing; a sad, nervous laugh that echoed strangely.

'Vile old woman, old fool,' he kept saying, trembling with anger and disgust. 'So then, we're going to pay her for her son . . . Do such creatures deserve any pity?'

I didn't reply and he closed his eyes, as he often did, weary all of a sudden.

I tried to imagine his thoughts. But when he opened his eyes, his face was impenetrable once more. I remember thinking about the elderly Jewess; her absurd gesture had revealed such depths of despair, ignorance and poverty. And on that day, I don't know why, but for the first time the idea of murdering this pompous fool filled me with horror.

17

A few days passed, and the story of the elderly Jewess began to bear bitter fruit. I don't know if it was because Courilof's sadness over the death of the prince was magnified by his anxiety over his own fate. I don't think so: he was too wrapped up in himself to realise how very useful the elderly man had been to him, how the prestige of Nelrode's name was enough to put an end to certain conspiracies against him. Nevertheless, around that time, on several occasions he would say: 'He was faithful to his friends. He was a loyal man, you could count on his word. That is very rare in life, young man . . . You'll see.'

If he still had any illusions, however, the arrival of the first anonymous letters quickly made them vanish.

Up until then, Dahl's fears of displeasing the prince had kept him from campaigning against the minister, whose post he desired for himself. With the prince gone, the game began.

Dahl rushed to tell everyone at court that the Minister of Education had been threatened by an elderly Jewess from Lodz with scandalous revelations about 'the beautiful Margot's past'.

'She used to live in Lodz, when she was a second-rate actress in a touring company,' Dahl said. 'This woman, a former midwife, had secretly given her an abortion, and after learning of Margot's excellent marriage, she had come to St Petersburg to blackmail the minister.' As proof, he pointed to the sum of money that Courilof had, in fact, sent to the old Jewess. Suddenly all the old stories about Marguerite Eduardovna resurfaced; they had been discreetly whispered around the city at the time of her marriage, and now they were openly discussed. Without a doubt, some of them were true, based entirely on fact; no one could deny her youthful indiscretions or her affair with Nelrode. Public opinion deemed it scandalous.

'An ugly, filthy business,' said Dahl in disgust.

They were saying that she still had lovers, protected by Courilof, as he himself had been protected by his predecessor: 'It's her good nature. She happily uses her great influence over her husband to protect her former lovers and numerous admirers in the two most prestigious regiments in the army, the Horseguards and the Preobrazhensky Guards.'

That, however, was partly true. But they also accused her of being the mistress of Hippolyte, Courilof's nephew, whom she couldn't stand; and, finally, of procuring young girls for her elderly husband, because she was 'a loving wife.' That was just as absurd as the rumour Fanny spread about 'the infamous orgies in the house at the Iles'.

I was truly astonished that anyone who actually knew the minister could believe such idle gossip. Poor Courilof – pious, conscientious, cowardly and prudent – was entirely incapable of carrying out such deeds. Nevertheless, he wasn't a man of 'flawless morals', as Froelich would have put it. Courilof's private life was as uneventful as any ordinary Swiss citizen's, but it probably hadn't always been that way. He was hot-blooded and extremely passionate. These days he no longer indulged himself, and hadn't for many years – undoubtedly due to religious scruples and because he had to be prudent. But he found it particularly odious to see his enemies guessing the secret weaknesses he forced himself to overcome. I was never able to understand one element of his character: a mixture of sincere puritanism and deceitfulness. As for the rest – well, I found him quite transparent.

After a while, the press got hold of the widow Aarontchik's story. The extreme right accused Courilof of 'liberalism', of 'giving in to revolutionary ideas', because he had given money to the mother of a suspicious Jew. On the other hand, revolutionary newspapers edited abroad reported that this woman's son had been murdered by policemen, agents provocateurs paid by Courilof, in order to destroy papers that might compromise the careers of certain highly placed members of the teaching profession.

The Emperor allowed it to continue. He hated Courilof, as much as such a weak man could experience any strong feelings. He'd heard details of certain unfortunate things his minister had said; he guessed that Courilof wished to one day see Grand Duke Michael, the Emperor's brother, on the throne. (Prince Alexis, heir to the throne, hadn't been born yet, but the Emperor and Empress had an unshakeable belief that they would one day have a son.)

Finally, owing to Courilof's regular tactlessness, he had a falling out with his colleague from the Home Office as well; its director could not forgive Courilof for having criticised one of his men. Morning, noon and night, masses of letters and newspapers from varying political affiliations landed on Courilof's desk; all of them hostile to him.

Marguerite Eduardovna did her best to remove them, but by some strange fate, despite all the precautions she took, every one landed in her husband's hands. He never read them in front of us and, sometimes, openly threw them away. But he couldn't prevent his gaze from immediately moving towards the title of the item underlined in blue pencil. He would gesture for one of the servants and say, 'Burn this filth.'

And as they collected up the scattered papers, he stared at the pages with burning curiosity. His large, pale eyes almost popping out of his head, he looked like an animal strangled by two strong hands, being choked to death. Finally, when the servant left, carrying away the stack of letters, Courilof would turn towards us and say: 'Dinner's ready! Come along!'

The children spoke quietly, but he remained silent, looking at each of us absent-mindedly, without actually seeing us; sometimes, he couldn't control the way his lips trembled slightly. He then spoke quickly, enunciating each word in a hateful, scornful manner, his voice growing more and more scathing and shrill. At other times, he fell into a deep dream, sighed, gently reached out to his son who sat at his side, and stroked his hair.

On those days, he was more patient and in a better mood than usual. He resigned himself to putting up with

the boiling hot compresses that Langenberg had ordered
me to place on his liver. It was as if he were offering his
physical pain up to God and asking in return that he
quash his enemies.

18

I went into his room every morning to treat him, as soon as he was awake. He was stretched out on a chaise-longue in front of the open window, wearing a scarlet silk dressing gown that made his cheeks look pale and puffy. For some time now, his wild beard had been going grey. The yellowish colour of his skin, the deep purple bags under his eyes and the two delicate bruises that appeared at the sides of his nose were evidence of the progress of his disease. He had lost weight, he was melting away; his heavy, yellowish flesh hung on him like a piece of over-sized clothing. This was obvious only when he was naked; once he was dressed, his uniform, with its decorations across his chest, became a kind of imaginary breast-plate.

It was obvious that Langenberg's hot compresses had about as much effect on his cancer as they would on a corpse.

Every morning, his son came to see him. He would hold the boy, stroke him, gently place his large hand on the boy's forehead, push his hair back, lightly pull his long ears. He treated him with deep and unique tenderness; he seemed afraid of hurting him, of touching him too roughly. But

then he would say, 'Just look at how strong he is, don't
you think, Monsieur Legrand? Off you go, my boy . . .'

With his daughter, the public Courilof re-emerged: cold,
impassive, giving orders without raising his voice. In spite
of myself, I felt an aversion to Irène Valerianovna. But I
liked the married couple, the Killer Whale and his old
tart; they moved me, I don't know why.

Now, as I write, I recall, I wander about, it remains
impossible for me to explain, even to myself, how I could
intimately understand these two people. Could it be
because I lived in an abstract world all my life, in a 'glass
cage'? For the first time, I saw human beings: unhappy
people with ambitions, faults, foolishness. But I haven't
got time to think about those things! I just want to concen-
trate on what happened back then, that moment buried
in my memory . . . Anything is better than sitting and
doing nothing, waiting to die. Look at the work done by
the Party: what Karl Marx brought to the workers, the
translations of Lenin's writings, the Communist Doctrine,
all doled out in instalments to the local Bolshevik middle
classes! I did what I could. But I'm ill, I'm tired of it all.
These old memories are less tiring. They numb me,
preventing my memory from lingering on futile recollec-
tions of war and conquest, on everything that will never
again return – at least, not for me.

I recall that Courilof went to the court one day around
that time, when some foreign sovereign or other notable
was there to be received. Courilof could hardly stand up:
two servants dressed him, flitting around him and pinning
his decorations on his chest, stuffing him into his dress
uniform. He wore a kind of corset that tied at the back,

to support the diseased portion of his body underneath his clothes. I was in the next room and could hear him panting in pain as they tightened the corset.

He got into the carriage, looking stiff and pompous, sparkling with gold. They left.

He came back around dusk; when I heard Marguerite Eduardovna scream, I immediately rushed out. I thought he'd passed out. He didn't get out of the car himself but rather was carried out by servants and brought to the house. To my great surprise, this relatively calm and patient man flew into a rage when one of the servants accidentally knocked against his arm, started swearing and hitting him.

The servant, who had a simple, kind face beneath the cap of his uniform, went white with terror and stood motionless, as if he were at attention, looking straight ahead. His wide, horrified eyes fixed on his master, with the same dumbfounded look you see in cattle.

Courilof seemed struck himself at the sound of his own slap. He stopped. I could see his lips moving, as the look on the valet's face rekindled his fury. He shook his fist, shouted, 'Get out of here, you good-for-nothing bastard!', let out a thunderous curse in Russian, then collapsed; he didn't actually faint, he just fell into a heap like an animal dying of rabies. His neck moved like a bull's does when it's trying to shake off the sharp spears digging into its flanks. He got up with great difficulty. Pushing us away, he staggered up the stairs. Marguerite Eduardovna and I followed him up to his room. He tore off his collar. He couldn't stop whimpering. It wasn't until he was in bed and his wife was stroking his forehead that he began to calm down. I left them like that: she sat at his bedside, talking to him quietly; he had his eyes closed, his entire face twitching nervously.

I thought he would want me to stay that night to keep an eye on him, as he always did when he was ill; but he seemed afraid he might say something he shouldn't. He didn't send for me. Only his wife stayed by his side.

When I saw her the next day, I asked about the minister's health. She made an effort to smile. 'Oh! It was nothing,' she said over and over again. 'It was nothing, nothing at all . . .'

She shook her head, her lips trembling, then looked straight at me with her deep, wide eyes. 'If only he could rest for a few months . . . We could go and live in Paris for a while . . . Paris, in the spring, when the chestnut trees are in bloom . . . Don't you think! Do you know Paris?'

She fell silent.

'Men are ambitious,' she said suddenly, with a sigh.

Later, I found out what happened when Courilof saw the Emperor at court; at least, I heard what Courilof's enemies were saying. The Emperor had received his minister while nervously fiddling with the pencils on his desk. This was how people close to him knew they had fallen from favour. When they arrived, before saying a word to them and without looking up, Nicolas II would start automatically arranging the files and other items on his desk.

Rumour had it that the Emperor had said, word for word: 'You know that I do not meddle in your private life, but you could at least try to avoid scandals.'

Later on, it occurred to me that the Emperor wouldn't

have needed to say even that much; his disapproval would have been infinitely more subtle, less obvious, perhaps barely visible to the naked eye, a hint of coldness in his voice, the Empress looking away . . .

The next day, someone mentioned the visit of the foreign sovereign in front of me.

'His Majesty deigned to forget I was there,' Courilof said bitterly. 'He failed to introduce me to the king.'

There was a silence. Everyone understood what that meant. In fact, for some time now, the Killer Whale's position had been precarious. A strange joy ran through me.

'Well, to hell with it!' I thought. 'Let him go away, let him give up his job as minister and live in peace until the cancer kills him!'

The idea of killing this man filled me with repulsion and horror. He was a blind creature already living in the shadow of death; his face looked ghostly, yet he was still preoccupied with vain dreams and futile ambitions. How many times during that period did he say over and over again: 'Russia will forget my enemies, but she will not forget me.'

It seemed strange, grotesque even, to think that he had already forgotten about the men who owed their deaths to his inability to give lucid orders in time; or to the system of espionage he had instituted. He still believed posterity would judge him by his good deeds, that posterity would be forced to choose between him, that bastard Dahl, and the rest of the other idiots!

I remember . . . We were sitting on a bench in the garden: Courilof, his wife and his daughter, who listened to him without really paying attention, her delicate, childlike face closed and impenetrable. You could tell she was very far away for the moment, in a day-dreaming world where worries about her father had no place. When he'd stopped talking, she continued to play absent-mindedly with the long gold necklace she wore. He turned, looked at her, and frowned sadly in annoyance. Little Ivan was running about, calling the dogs; you could hear him panting; he was fat and easily became short of breath.

I watched thick clouds of mosquitoes rise above the dark waters in the bay. Everyone around me seemed just like those mosquitoes; they hovered over the marshes, restless in the wind, tormenting people, only to disappear, the devil knows why!

19

Irène Valerianovna's birthday was in June. Towards the middle of the month, they began to prepare for the ball at Courilof's house. The minister wanted to invite the Emperor and Empress in order to show his enemies that, in spite of everything, he was solidly established in his post and loved at court. No one was completely blind to his scheme, but it did, nevertheless, make a good impression.

The Emperor's coldness had not yet been followed by any hostile acts towards his minister. A large sum of money had silenced the reactionary press a bit; as for the liberal newspapers, they continued moaning, but to Courilof, they were of no consequence.

I thought that Marguerite Eduardovna was going to leave St Petersburg before the ball. Every day I expected to see her go; but no, she stayed, though not to take care of the arrangements. It was the minister himself who took care of all the preparations. His complexion was pale; he looked at everyone and everything anxiously, with a harsh and defiant expression on his face.

One day I took a chance and again followed Dahl and the Killer Whale into the garden, where they were talking.

Dahl looked his most evil self. He watched Courilof in silence, a smirk on his thin, tight lips.

At one point I think they heard me behind them: the gravel was crunching beneath my feet. Courilof seemed impatient. But as soon as they were sitting down, I hid behind the manicured hedges and kept still. They forgot about me.

'My dear Valerian Alexandrovitch,' I heard Dahl say. 'Since you do not wish to offend your family and acquaintances by excluding them, and as it would be unacceptable, on the other hand, to expect Their Majesties to mingle with your relatives and friends, why don't you organise an entertainment in the Malachite Room, just for the princes, the very high aristocracy and the ladies?'

'Do you think so?' the Killer Whale said, sounding doubtful.

'Yes I do.'

'Perhaps . . . Yes, it's an ingenious solution . . . Perhaps.'

They fell silent.

'My dear friend,' Courilof began.

Dahl nodded, smiling. 'I am completely at your service, my friend.'

'You know that Their Majesties have not come to my house since my first wife died.'

'Since your second marriage, yes, I know, my friend.'

'To invite them, now, I feel . . . would be rather difficult. I . . . Who could I send to put out feelers? What do you think? I have a list of women who specialise in this type of mission. On the other hand, I've heard that Her Imperial Highness hardly ever goes out at present; it would be very painful, as you can imagine, to suffer a refusal.'

He read the names on his list to Dahl. At each one, Dahl interrupted him with a little snigger, gently touching his arm: 'No . . . no . . . not her . . . Her behaviour . . . His Majesty expressed disapproval of her . . . That one is divorced, and the suggestion of immorality in her actions, even though she might have been wrongly accused, has upset Her Imperial Highness. You simply would not believe, my friend, the extent to which the court is leaning towards a sense of austerity that borders on puritanism. Do you understand?'

'I understand.'

The baron said no more and looked at the Killer Whale with an expression that was both severe and mocking.

'It's the trend, my friend.' He shrugged his shoulders. Each of his looks seemed to say: *You do see what I mean*; his smile looked as though it meant: *You can guess, I suppose, to whom I am referring, to the fragility of your position.*

Carefully lowering their voices, they started talking about Courilof's daughter as a possible wife for the young Anatole Dahl.

'An alliance between us would be valuable,' said Courilof, sounding sly and frightened. 'I like your son . . . Of course, they're still children.'

'Yes,' said Dahl, coldly. 'He's a good boy. But he's very young and so innocent! He needs some time to experience life, to sow his wild oats.' He said this last bit in French, forcing a little laugh.

'Of course, of course,' murmured Courilof. 'Nevertheless . . .'

His words were measured, full of tact and paternal

dignity; but how much fear, how much impatience made
him shudder inside. He was, quite simply, offering Dahl his
daughter as if she were a sacrifice to the angry gods. I knew
that the young woman was extremely wealthy: the first
Madame Courilof had left her entire fortune to her children; and the minister too had handed over his own portion
to them when he had married Marguerite Eduardovna. I
have never known anyone as clumsy in his generosity.

Dahl's unexpected reservations about a potential
marriage confirmed to me that his attitude towards
Courilof was firmly entrenched, even more so than
Courilof thought. I remember that I was listening attentively when suddenly, I threw my head back and looked
out at the peaceful bay, up at the sky. I felt an extraordinary hunger for an insignificant, bourgeois, peaceful life,
far from the rest of the world.

Nevertheless, Dahl and the Killer Whale finally agreed
on the name of some woman or other, a friend of the
Empress.

'She's a good woman and is experienced at such
missions,' said Dahl.

Courilof sighed. 'Do you really think Their Majesties
will deign to come?'

'I'll see what I can do,' Dahl promised, wearily and
rather regally shaking his head.

'Alas! I do not have the good fortune of being in favour
with my venerable Empress.'

'Of course you do, of course you do,' the baron
muttered. 'Her Majesty is a woman, after all' (he seemed
to be apologising, by a slight hesitation in his voice, for
attaching such a common word to the sacred name of the

Empress); 'she is highly strung, with a very Germanic frankness, unable to keep her thoughts to herself. She has a good heart: too good, perhaps, too noble, for the petty concerns of our times.'

'Of course,' Courilof replied warmly. 'No one, if I may say so' (this way of expressing himself seemed to please him), 'no one in the world adores and reveres Her Imperial Majesty as I do. Nevertheless, Mathieu Iliitch, I do believe that she does not like me. I must have offended her, without meaning to, I assure you, or perhaps hurt her feelings. Being a queen does not make her less of a woman, as you have so rightly said.'

'Sometimes, it's even regrettable,' Dahl hissed, his voice full of insinuation.

Then they began to exchange views on various members of the court and the sovereigns. The conversation lasted rather a long time.

'Mathieu Iliitch,' Courilof suddenly said, 'you are the one whom Her Majesty has judged worthy of reporting certain of her thoughts to me, regarding the presence of my wife at the ball. Would you please be so kind as to tell her . . .'

He stopped for a moment and I could hear his voice breaking, a tremor of fear and courage beneath his pompous statements.

'Please could you tell her that Marguerite Eduardovna, that *my wife*, will not be leaving St Petersburg and that she will not do so until she has paid her respects to her sovereigns?'

Dahl hesitated for a split second. 'Absolutely, my dear friend.'

'I'm tired of all this uncertainty. I wish *my wife*' (once again, he stressed the words), '*my wife* to be treated by everyone with the respect that my own name should guarantee her. I have thought about this for a long time, Mathieu Iliitch. If I give in this time, it will start all over again in some other way. I know very well that the persecution from which I am suffering began the day when I insisted on presenting my wife at court. I know that . . . But I wish the situation to be clear. If the Emperor refuses to come, I will know that it is impossible for me to remain in my post. I would happily resign; I'm ill, I'm tired.'

A long silence followed.

'All right, my dear friend,' Dahl said again.

Then they parted. Dahl left; Courilof remained sitting on the bench, two feet away from me. I could see him perfectly clearly.

It was a hot, hazy day; those small flies you get in summer were buzzing around. Courilof's face was pale and still. At one point he let out a long, deep sigh that sounded as if it came truly from the very depths of his heart. I watched him for a long time. Finally, he stood up. He walked slowly to the end of the small path, flicking at the gravel in front of him with the end of his cane; he looked weary and pensive. But as soon as he came to the wide, straight road that led to the house, my Courilof stood up tall, stuck out his chest, and continued along with a stiff, pompous stride. It was the posture of a man accustomed to walking through two rows of people as they bowed down.

20

Over the next few days, the house began to resemble a buzzing hive. Partitions were knocked down, wall hangings nailed up.

As far as I can remember, the Empress made everyone wait a long time for a response. Courilof became more and more nervous. From morning until night, he paced back and forth through the house, his heavy footsteps resonating against the parquet flooring. He was impatient, behaved harshly towards his secretaries and servants. I especially recall his hostility and indifference when he spoke to his daughter. Sometimes he furtively watched Marguerite Eduardovna. I imagined he was contemplating the importance of his political ambitions, comparing them to his love for her. Each time, he wore a kind of resigned smile, an expression of profound gentleness; then he would turn away and sigh.

Meanwhile, Fanny waited for me every night at the little gate to the grounds and told me about the harassment in the universities, the disturbances crushed with unbelievable violence, the students who'd been arrested and deported. I remember a strange feeling: her voice shook with hatred while Courilof's pale face haunted me. There was no difference. The students were right; so was Courilof. Every human insect thought only of himself: of his pathetic, threatened existence, hated and scorned by everyone else. It was legitimate . . . but I understood them all too well. There were no rules any more. God demands blind faith from his creations.

More time passed and still the Empress did not reply. Nevertheless, there was a continual rush of florists and upholsterers to the house. For some time, they had discussed organising a celebration at night in the gardens.

As I said, the grounds in front of the house led down to the water, a sad little northern bay, surrounded by pine trees and brambles. Courilof, it seemed, wanted to build a stage and have costumed musicians performing. But all these niceties were completely alien to his nature. His nephew, Hippolyte Courilof, was helping him. Courilof never knew his nephew's reputation, nor how badly it reflected on him. He did his best to help the boy advance in his career. It was mainly because of him that Courilof was accused of nepotism, to the detriment of the State.

'*He* doesn't steal,' people said, 'but it's us ordinary people who lose out. He gets posts for all his close relatives, his cousins, his brothers, and *they* all steal!'

The first Madame Courilof had raised the boy, who'd been orphaned very young, and the minister scrupulously continued to carry out all his dead wife's former wishes. In his first wife's room, which remained intact, was an enormous portrait of Hippolyte Courilof as a child, his long, pallid face framed by a mass of golden curls. It was part of the minister's character, this foolish loyalty, his unswerving honesty; such actions eased his conscience, but also led him to commit masses of blunders that caused enormous fiascos.

Every evening, he and the minister would go down to the riverbank together, to measure the land, discuss where the musicians should set up, or the colour of the paper lanterns.

Hippolyte Nicolaévitch ran along the water's edge, waving his arms, pointing to the bay.

'Just picture it, uncle, the sea in the distance, lit up in the moonlight, the delicious perfume of the flowers, the music, muted by the water, the women in their beautiful dresses, a true Watteau painting!'

He pronounced the letter 'r' deeply, as they do in French, raising his chubby white hands up high. He was a hunch-back without the hump; his chest was extremely round and his long, pale face sat low on his neck.

'It will be very expensive, of course,' he added casually. 'Leave it to me.'

Dusk was extraordinarily desolate in these sad islands. I remember the falling rain splashing against the calm surface of the bay. The setting sun hovered above the horizon until morning, a circle of dull, smoky red, engulfed in mist.

Courilof listened gloomily and often called out to me: 'What do you think, Monsieur Legrand? You don't say much, but you have good taste. What colour do you think the paper lanterns should be? Green?'

He didn't listen to what I said, though; he just stood there watching the still water and then walked back, sighing.

Finally, Courilof decided to go and ask for the Emperor's reply himself and give him the guest list for approval, if he agreed to attend. I accompanied the minister to the Winter Palace that day. When he got into the carriage, he saw all the people who'd come to ask favours waiting in the courtyard. They'd been there since morning; the rain had pushed them back under an awning, like a herd of sheep. When the Killer Whale appeared, they hesitantly took three steps forward. The minister waved his hand wearily. Two servants appeared.

'Out! Get going!'

In a flash, they had pushed the masses of waiting people back and closed the gate. Courilof, gloomy and preoccupied, got into the carriage, gesturing for me to follow him. It was rather funny: he too got a bad reception that day . . . the Emperor was tired; the Empress was ill . . .

I waited for a long time in front of the palace, in the stifling heat of the enclosed little carriage. Then we retraced our steps back to the Iles.

He huddled in the corner, silently staring into space. Sometimes he would tell the driver to go faster by making a dry little clicking noise, but as soon as the horses began to gallop, he'd get annoyed and swear at the coachman. Then we'd slow down again. It was raining harder and harder. It's strange how well I understood the Killer Whale's 'feelings'. And still, it was difficult to guess the emotions that ran through him beneath his armour, his stony look. I sensed his emotions in a strange way, one that gave me both a feeling of satisfaction and a kind of contentment that was almost physical. Later on, when I escaped from prison in Siberia, I used to hunt for food along the road;

as I stalked my prey, I remember sensing it quiver in the same way.

The heat, a steamy torrent, seemed to rise up from the earth. He was clearly dying to talk to me; but the poor fool was always afraid that a single look or gesture would be enough to give him away. 'We're just slaves in fancy clothing,' he finally said, bitterly.

I didn't reply, and he also fell silent, looked away to watch the waves of rain streaming down the windows. We'd gone past St Petersburg's city limits. We took a large avenue lined with trees; their leaves were soaking wet and the raindrops fell from them noisily, with a sharp, metallic sound.

At one point, the horse shied. I glanced at Courilof. For a man who was usually absolutely in control of himself, every shout in the street, jolt or the sound of glass shattering made him wince involuntarily. Almost immediately afterwards, his face would freeze into a look of icy calm. I felt something akin to pleasure in witnessing these nervous reactions, as they proved he was obsessed with the thought of being assassinated.

That day, he noticed nothing. He didn't stiffen; his body swayed with the carriage's movements as it was thrown to one side, veered off course by a stone. When I asked, 'Did that hurt?' he seemed to awaken from a dream. I could see his pale, sagging face, his half-closed eyes.

'No,' he said.

Then he shook his head.

'It's strange. I feel better. I feel less pain when my mind is on all these problems.'

I said nothing.

'The higher a man's position,' he sighed, 'the heavier it seems the cross he must bear.'

'But you're tired, aren't you?' I said. 'Why don't you retire? Marguerite Eduardovna . . .'

He cut in. 'I can't. This is my life.'

He fell silent and we continued on our way home.

The idea of music along the riverbank had been abandoned. Courilof decided to have the entertainment in the Malachite Room, as Dahl had suggested. The Emperor and Empress had ended up vaguely agreeing to come, but it was possible they might cancel at any time. Nevertheless, the invitations were sent out.

The Malachite Room took up half of the first floor; it was here that a stage was set up. A few days before the ball, I went in and found Courilof watching one of the rehearsals. A young woman was dressed as a shepherdess in the style of Louis XV; she was playing an antique instrument, a sort of bagpipe that made the sharp, shrill sound of a fife. All the furniture had been removed; all that remained was the enormous Venetian glass chandelier, its crystals chiming to echo the music.

Courilof listened, his wide, pale eyes almost popping out of his head. He paid his compliments to the musician, and finally the woman left. We stood alone in the middle of the stage. I noticed with surprise that the bare boards used to make the stage had been badly assembled. They looked as if they might collapse under the slightest weight. I pointed this out to Courilof. He looked through me, as though coming out of a trance, and said nothing.

'Look at how flimsy this is,' I said again.

All of a sudden, he clenched his teeth; a look of blind

fury came over his face. 'Well, that's fine! Just fine! Lord! If only they would all go to hell! Disappear into a hole in the ground!' He pulled himself together but still seemed worried. 'Don't take any notice of me, I'm not well, I'm nervous.'

He walked away from me, went over to the window, looked outside for a long time without saying a word, then left the room.

21

As I recall, the ball was at the end of June.

That night, I went out for a walk through the Iles. I liked those clear nights. I could see the royal carriages, one after the other, driving down the wide avenues. I caught a glimpse of the most extraordinary faces through the carriage windows: women with thin, pinched features, covered in jewels, like religious relics, tiaras shimmering on their foreheads; men whose uniforms gleamed strangely, speckled with diamonds and gold. The odd light cast by the summer night made them look like ghosts from a dream.

Afterwards, when I was head of the Special Police, I remember I used to interrogate suspects on such nights; they were brought to me in groups and then executed at dawn. I can picture their pale faces, the evening light that fell on their features, their eyes staring into mine. Some of them were so exhausted that they seemed indifferent to everything; they answered my questions with a weary little sneer. Very few of them fought for their lives. They just allowed themselves to be taken away and massacred without saying a word. A revolution is such a slaughterhouse! Is it really worth it? Nothing's really worth the trouble; it's true, not even life.

I walked towards the gardens, opened the gate and immediately ran into Courilof. He had come outside to check on the police surrounding the house. Everywhere you turned was a policeman in civilian clothing hiding behind a tree.

'What are you doing out here, Monsieur Legrand? Come inside, you'll see how wonderful everything looks.' He forced me to go back into the house. Through the open windows, I could see the dazzling lights in the Malachite Room shining down brightly on the women fluttering their fans; in the front row were the Emperor and the princes.

Courilof looked up and listened for a moment, frowning. 'Can you hear that?' he said quietly. 'Bach.'

The calm, heavy music seemed to float very high above us. I listened with him. The famous R . . . was playing. I do not really like music, since I am not really interested in the arts in general. I only enjoy Bach and Haydn.

'Their Highnesses have arrived,' Courilof said. 'This is undoubtedly the first time you've seen them, isn't it? There's the Empress and, beside her, the Emperor himself. What venerable nobility shines from the faces of these absolute masters of our great Russia,' he continued, adopting his usual solemn tone that simultaneously annoyed and touched me.

Through the bright glass partition, he pointed out Nicolas II; he was facing us, listening attentively. Once, during a slight pause in the music, I could distinctly hear the Emperor give a weary little cough; then I saw him raise his gloved hand to his lips and lower his head.

'Let me stay out here,' I said to Courilof. 'I can't breathe in these large reception rooms.'

He left me and went back inside. The night was oppressively still, and every now and then there were flashes of lightning. I saw the crowd stand up; I heard the sound of footsteps and the clash of sabres against the parquet floor. The princes were going into the next room, where supper was being served. I kept walking back and forth beneath the windows. I saw the Emperor with a glass of champagne in his hand and Ina in a white dress. Marguerite Eduardovna was wearing a corsage of roses with a fan of diamonds pinned into her hair; there were many other people as well, a mass of strange faces.

I was having difficulty breathing; the air was absolutely still. As I turned the corner, I ran into one of the policemen; he had seen me talking to the minister and didn't bother me. All he did was follow me for a while along the path, absent-mindedly, out of habit. I offered him a cigarette, calling out to him, 'You've got your work cut out for you tonight, haven't you?'

He frowned. 'The house is well guarded,' he said cautiously, hesitantly, in French; he had a heavy German accent.

He touched his hat and disappeared into the shadows.

It was strange to be walking through the garden like this, spied on by the police. At the time, I didn't often think about my own life. I existed in a kind of waking dream that was both lucid and confusing. On that night, for the first time, I thought about myself, about the death that awaited me. But truthfully, it was hard for me to care . . . I remember thinking: 'I have to get hold of some bombs, not a gun, so I can also be blown up.' It was truly strange to be telling myself that the minister and I would probably die together ... I felt a burning sensation rise through my body. I find storms oppressive, and the heavy weather that comes just before them is even worse ... It was choking me. Once again I thought: 'If I could just close my eyes, go to sleep.' What a rotten life ... Incomprehensible. It's easy to kill people you don't know, like the men who were marched past me those nights in 1919, and afterwards ... And even they ...

I had interrogated them: 'What's your name? Where were you born?' I'd look at their papers and passports; whether they were real or forged, they evoked the image of a life that was meaningful, almost fraternal. 'You, the thief, the speculator, the dealer who provided the Imperial Army with worn-out leather boots, rotten food, you're not a bad person, you wanted the money, that's all. You lean towards me again, passionately, hopefully: "Comrade, I have dollars ... Comrade, take pity on me; I've never hurt anyone; I have young children; take pity on me!" Tomorrow, when two men blow your brains out in some dark shed, will you even know what you died for?'

I remember the thugs in the White Army who hung peasants by the thousands; they burned the villages they passed through so completely that the only thing left in the houses was the empty space where the stoves had been. As they were dying, they looked at me with their stunned, bloodshot eyes: 'Superintendent, comrade, why, why are you making me suffer like this? I've never done anything wrong.' It was ... farcical ... And it was the same with Courilof.

'Eliminate the unjust for the good of the majority.'
Why should we? And who is just? And how do people
treat me? It is unbearable for a hunter to kill an animal
he has looked after and fed. But all the same, as long as
we are on this earth, we have to play the game. I killed
Courilof. I sent men to their deaths whom I realised, in
a moment of lucidity, were like my brothers, like my very
soul . . .

I had a moment of madness that evening. It was another
one of those stormy, oppressive nights. I abandoned the
old, futile pile of papers and went down into the garden;
for a long time, I paced up and down the small path, ten
feet long, that leads to the wall and the road beyond. I
was overwhelmed by thirst. Anger surged inside me, and
I felt as if I were being strangled by a heavy, rough hand.
In the morning, the rain finally came, and I was able to
stretch out on my bed and fall asleep.

*I'm coughing now, can't catch my breath. Not a single
sound in the house. I like this irrevocable solitude.*

And so, there you have it: one summer's evening thirty
years ago, I walked back and forth beneath Courilof's
windows and watched that crowd of dazzling clowns, all
of whom are now dead.

Time passed. It was time for the Emperor to leave. His
carriage arrived. In the shadow of the trees, all the
policemen moved forward, forming an invisible circle. I
tried to see if I could hear anything: you could vaguely
make out the sound of their breathing and see their feet
brushing against the grass. The minister, bare-headed,
accompanied the Emperor, as was the tradition; he held
a large golden candelabra with lit candles, even though

the night was perfectly clear. A respectful crowd bustled behind them.

As soon as the Emperor began to speak, there was absolute silence. I could clearly hear his hesitant little cough and his words: 'Thank you. It was a wonderful ball.'

He got into the carriage next to the Empress; she sat upright and stiff, mechanically nodding her sad, haughty head. She wore long white feathers in her hair and a wide necklace of various precious gemstones. They left.

Courilof was beaming. An eager crowd of people surrounded him, complimenting him, as if some part of His Royal Highness had remained glued to him. He pointed to the gardens.

'Ladies, would you enjoy walking beneath these arches?' he said, with the pompous tone he used on his best days.

He turned to Dahl and took his arm. They followed the crowd of people who were walking along the paths.

'I must congratulate you,' Dahl said. 'His Majesty was more than kind.'

Courilof was walking on clouds. Soon the musicians, hidden by the shrubbery, began to play. Torches had been lit and set into the ground around the lawns; their flames cast a deep red glow. The reflected light on the deathly pale faces of Dahl and Courilof looked like shimmering blood; they had the same pale faces you find on the people of St Petersburg who never see the sunshine, just the artificial light of their summer nights (they sleep during the day). It was rather appropriate, when you think about it.

Dahl took the minister's arm and squeezed it affectionately. It was then that I guessed the Killer Whale's end was near.

'I just knew that if Their Majesties got to know my wife a bit better,' Courilof said, 'they would realise that what they had been led to believe was incorrect.' He smiled proudly. That's what this man was like. His mind was certainly not as impressive as he thought, but it was greater than I myself had first believed. Yet the moment everything was going well for him, he became confused. Success went to his head like wine.

I went back to my room. I opened the window, watching the carriages in the courtyard move off, one after the other. I listened to the sound of accordions playing in the stables until morning. I saw the light for a moment in Marguerite Eduardovna's bedroom, then everything went dark.

22

A week after the ball, the Emperor sent for Courilof. Very politely – for Emperor Nicolas was an enlightened sovereign who, unlike his father, never displayed any brutality in his words or deeds – he informed his minister that he must choose between disgrace or divorce; he urged him to opt for the latter. But Courilof refused to leave his wife; he even displayed a sense of indignation in the matter that the Emperor found 'tactless', as he would later say. Courilof was relieved of his official duties.

I saw my Courilof return from St Petersburg that day. His face seemed as impassive as ever, just the tiniest bit greyer, the corners of his mouth sagging slightly more. But he seemed perfectly calm and in control of himself; he smiled with an ironic, resigned expression that surprised me.

'Now I'll be able to rest as long as I like, Monsieur Legrand, my friend,' he said as he walked past me.

His dishonour was meant to be kept secret for a while; but the 'upper circles' in St Petersburg, as the court and its members were referred to at the time, openly talked about it.

At first Courilof's composure surprised me. Later on, I realised he hadn't actually understood the extent of his fall from grace. He undoubtedly believed it would be temporary . . . or perhaps his deep conviction that he had *behaved like a gentleman*, as he liked to put it, tensing his lips and hissing in that particular way I'd come to know so well, perhaps that was some consolation to him . . . Nor was he unhappy to have spoken to his beloved sovereign alone, for the first time in his life.

The rebels at court warmly congratulated him on his attitude; he thus enjoyed a brief popularity that deceived him and made his head spin. But it was short-lived. Soon he was alone. Forgotten. From my window, I started to watch him pace back and forth across his room in the evening, for hours on end. Gradually he became more irritable and miserable, locking himself away in his bedroom, all alone.

One day I went into his room. He was sitting at his desk; he was holding open a bronze box that contained a bundle of papers; he re-read them, then carefully folded them up, as if they were old love letters. They were all the telegrams he'd received when he'd been appointed Minister of Education; he always kept them with him, locked up in his desk.

When he saw me, he became a little flustered. I expected him to send me on my way with the same severe gesture he used to dismiss anyone who annoyed him, the regal turn of his head, as if to say, 'What is it? What do you want?' accompanied by an icy, heavy look in his pale blue eyes. But all he did was sadly tense his lips.

'Vanity of vanities, Monsieur Legrand, everything on this

earth is but ashes and vanity. One amuses oneself however one can at my age,' he added, trying in vain to sound indifferent. 'Honours are the baby rattles of the elderly.'

He thought for a moment and closed the drawer. Finally he gestured to me, inviting me to sit down next to him. He talked to me about Bismarck, whom he'd known. 'I met him; I went to visit the great man once; he was dismissed by an ungrateful ruler, like me . . . He lived alone, with his mastiff dogs . . . Being idle is deadly . . .'

He stopped for a moment, sighed: 'Power is a delectable poison . . . To some people,' he hastened to add, 'to *other* people . . . As for me, well, I've always been philosophical.'

He forced a slight, ironic smile, the way the dead Prince Nelrode used to do. But his wide, pale eyes stared into mine with a very human look of sadness and anxiety.

July finally came and went. I received my order to kill Courilof on 3 October. The Emperor of Germany was going to visit the tsar that day. A performance was being given at the Marie Theatre. The bomb had to be thrown as they came outside, not in the theatre itself, to avoid any accidents; still, it had to be early enough for the public and foreign dignitaries to see the assassination happen before their very eyes.

I'd been called to St Petersburg by Fanny. She was living in a kind of attic, above the dark canals of the Fontanka, in a room she shared with a family of workers.

I remember how hot it was that summer's day and the blinding limestone dust that flew up from the scaffolding, lit up by the blazing sun. We were alone in her room. I told her I wanted to see one of the leaders of the Party.

She didn't reply at first, then stared at me with her narrow, gleaming eyes.

'And just who would you like to see?' she finally asked.

I didn't know. I insisted.

'Your orders are to see no one.'

I was getting annoyed and insisted again. We parted without having agreed on anything.

A few days passed; she called for me to come to her place again one evening. I crossed the rickety little wooden entrance, past the banister that led to her room; then a man opened her door, came towards me, and shook my hand. A small lamp, hanging on the wall, gave off such a dim light that all I could make out of him was a wide-brimmed hat. His voice was rather strange, dry and sarcastic. His careful economy with words convinced me that he was used to speaking in public.

'We can't go in,' he said, shrugging lazily, wearily, in the direction of the room. 'There's a woman asleep in there, ill or drunk. I'm . . .' (He told me his name. This famous terrorist has since died, executed by the Soviets, whose bitter enemy he'd become in 1918.)

It was true; I could hear a woman moaning, interspersed with hiccoughs and groans.

'You wanted to speak to me,' he continued.

And he didn't even lower his voice in that hallway full of drunks, beggars, prostitutes leaving to go to work, half-naked kids who rushed past like rats. They walked by, staring at us, and pushed us out of the way. The man leaned against the banister and looked down at the dark shaft of the stairwell. That was where Courilof's fate was to be decided.

I said I didn't want to kill the minister. He didn't protest, just sighed wearily, like Courilof did when his secretary came to ask for additional information about a letter he had to finish.

'All right, fine, we'll find someone else.'

A drunk started singing in one of the filthy hovels. The man banged impatiently on the wall.

'So then . . . Shall we go downstairs?'

I stopped him again, and then . . . Ah! I can't remember what I said any more, but it felt like I was fighting for my brother's life.

'Why? What's the point? He's just a poor fool; if you get rid of him, the next one won't be any better, nor the one after.'

'I know,' he said, infuriated, 'I know. It will start all over again; you know very well we're not killing a man, we're killing the regime.'

I shrugged my shoulders. I felt a kind of embarrassment, as usual, afraid I might burst into the kind of pompous speech I so hated. But I simply said, 'Do you want to punish someone who is guilty, or remove the cause of the trouble, the problem, someone you consider dangerous?'

He became more thoughtful. He half sat on the flimsy little banister, steadied himself and whistled softly.

'The latter, of course.'

'He's finished. It's not been made official. But he's about to be replaced.'

He swore in a low, muffled voice.

'Again! The animal's already been caught! And when will it be made official?'

I gestured that I didn't know.

'Listen,' he said quickly, 'the third of October is the date set. Remember that there are going to be strikes in all the universities in October. There will be riots. Many students will die if Courilof remains in power. If we get rid of him, we'll terrify his successor and save many lives that are far more valuable than that inhuman machine.'

'What if he's resigned from office by October third?' I asked.

'Well, too bad then,' he replied. 'What can we do? He'll be left alone. Otherwise, you understand, whether it's you or someone else . . .'

He didn't finish. The drunk began singing again in a plaintive voice. Fanny crept into the hallway.

'Leave, now; the spy is coming.'

We went downstairs together. The man walked quickly; I could see he wanted to leave before me so I wouldn't be able to see his face, but I got ahead of him and quickly looked at him. He was a young man, but worn out, and with gentle eyes. He looked at me, surprised.

'Listen, the bottom line is,' I said rapidly, 'it's a dirty business; don't you sometimes wish you could say to hell with it all and get out?'

I don't know why, but while I was looking at him, I felt something dramatic, something intense in our conversation.

He frowned. 'No, I have no pity whatsoever,' he said, responding to my thoughts rather than my words, as if he could read my mind. 'Those people deserve no more pity than mad dogs.'

I smiled in spite of myself, recognising Langenberg's words.

'You don't understand,' he continued haughtily. 'You emerged from your glass cage wrapped in cotton wool; you should have asked your father.'

'It's got nothing to do with pity,' I said. 'It's more that we seem to lack a kind of sense of humour . . . as do our enemies, for that matter . . . Don't you think?'

He looked at me thoughtfully. 'You have to make a choice, don't you? On October third!'

He said it again. I'd got the message and told him so. He smiled, nodding.

'You'll see; as soon as you have a bomb wrapped in your handkerchief or a gun in your trouser pocket and you see all those beaming people with their medals and fine decorations, the quiver that runs down your spine will be the ultimate reward. I've killed two of them.'

He tapped his hat and disappeared. After he left me, I roamed the streets of St Petersburg, the same three streets around the dark canal, until morning.

23

Almost imperceptibly, Courilof changed, growing sombre and anxious. At this time of year, he and his wife normally went to their house in the Caucasus or in France. But this year, it didn't even occur to him to leave. I don't know what he was expecting to happen. He didn't even know himself. Probably he thought that the Emperor would change his mind . . . or that the world would grind to a halt since he, Courilof, was no longer a minister.

Finally, towards the end of July, the Emperor's decree appeared, naming Dahl as successor to Courilof. He bore the blow without flinching, but he seemed to age very quickly. I noticed that his wife's presence weighed heavily on him. He was even more attentive and polite to her, but you could sense that she was a constant reminder to him of how he had sacrificed his career, and that memory was painful to him. The children, Ina and Ivan, were away – spending the summer somewhere in the Orel region with their aunt, as they did every year.

It seemed as if only my presence was bearable to the Killer Whale. I think it was because I walked very quietly, and he found my silence comforting. I have always walked as lightly and silently as possible.

The house had become as empty and hollow as an abandoned beehive. Quite naturally, no one came to see the disgraced minister any more, afraid of compromising themselves; but what astonished me was the surprise and hurt he seemed to feel because of this. In the morning, he would shout regally, 'My post!' It echoed through the entire house.

The servant would bring a few letters. Courilof would eagerly look at them, then throw them down on his bed, rifle through them and sigh. His face remained impassive; only his fingers trembled slightly.

'No message from the Emperor? Nothing?'

As he asked, he blushed visibly, emphasising his icy expression even more. You could tell that the question itself was painful, but that he couldn't help asking it. I remember the blood inching slowly up his face, colouring his pale features, right up to his high forehead. He jumped every time the bell rang, every time he heard a carriage passing in the street.

The weather was hot and beautiful. Courilof often went out in the garden early, breathing in the perfume of the flowers, of the great lawns covered in a sea of grass, like a prairie. They were cut at this time of year; you could hear the hissing of the scythe and the peasants' voices carrying through the peaceful air.

'Cut down just like us, Monsieur Legrand, just like us!' He stopped; looked around him, over towards the gulf, pale grey beneath the blue sky.

'It's easier to breathe this pure air; it hasn't been polluted yet by the stench of men. Don't you agree, Monsieur Legrand?'

He stabbed a leaf with the end of his cane, then raised it up to the light, stopping to look at the grass and the shrubs without seeing them, his heart heavy. He started to say how much the singing birds delighted him, but then his face contorted with pain.

'That's enough; let's go back! I can't bear their chirping! The sun is making my head spin,' he added, pointing to the pale northern sun reflected in the water.

It was the time of day when he used to report to the Emperor.

'*Cincinnatus . . . Let us begin to work our plough . . .*' Whenever he mentioned the Emperor or the Empress, the court or the ministers, he let out a short little snigger. As he stood beneath the stinging whip of adversity, this man – whom I had never known to be either spiritual or bitter – now voiced rather cruel and amusing verdicts on both people and things.

'Didn't you ever come across revolutionary immigrants in Switzerland?' he asked me once.

Fearing a trap, I replied: 'No.'

'Fanatics, cranks, villains!'

But, all in all, they scarcely interested him. What counted for him, for his sovereign, for Russia, were the plots of the grand dukes, the ministers and, most especially, the conspiracies and schemes of Dahl and his cohorts. He was their victim; he called them 'diabolical' and thought they were poisonous. He never spoke to me about it: I wasn't meant to know anything. I was nothing but an insignificant doctor, unworthy of sharing the destiny and misfortunes of the great men of this world. But in spite of himself, everything he said led back to what had happened to him.

My poor Courilof! I had never been as close to him, never understood him so well, despised him so much, felt as sorry for him as I did on those days, those nights. The pale, clear nights lasted twelve hours on the horizon, then began to darken, for it was August; in this climate it was already autumn, an arid, sad season everywhere, but especially here. I advised him to leave. I talked to him about Switzerland and a house in Vevey, a white house with a climbing red vine, like the Bauds' house . . . I drew the most idyllic pictures for him. In vain. He clung to his proximity to the Emperor, to his memories, to the illusion of power.

'Ministers, puppets,' he repeated furiously, over and over again. 'An Emperor? No, a saint! God preserve us from such saints on the throne! Everything in its proper place! As for the Empress!'

He stopped, pinching his lips into a scornful pout and sighed deeply. 'What I need is something to do . . .'

He needed something else as well: the illusion of influencing people's fate. You never get tired of that; otherwise, you're finished . . . completely finished . . . I know that now.

'You're the only one who's remained faithful to this old, disgraced man,' he said to me one day.

I made some vague reply. He sighed, then looked at me oddly, in that charming way of his.

'All in all,' he remarked, 'you're something of a mystery.'
'Why?' I said.

It gave me a certain sense of pleasure to ask.

'Why?' he repeated slowly. 'I don't know.'

At that very moment, I knew that some doubt had

crossed his mind. It was unbelievable to see how truly bizarre and obtuse these people were: they deported and imprisoned masses of innocent people and poor fools, but the really dangerous enemies of the regime slipped through their nets unharmed. Yes, at that moment, and for the first time, Courilof was suspicious. His uneasiness probably affected his reasoning. But without a doubt, he thought he had nothing left to fear; or perhaps he felt the same things towards me as I did towards him: understanding, curiosity, a vague kind of fraternity, pity, scorn ... How could I know? Perhaps he wasn't thinking anything of the sort . . . He shrugged his shoulders slightly and said nothing.

We went back to the house to have lunch with Marguerite Eduardovna, the three of us sitting around a table that was meant for twenty. During the meal, he was so irritable it verged on madness. One day, he smashed one of the Sèvres vases that decorated the table; he threw it at the butler's head, I don't remember why now. It was pink, made of soft-paste porcelain, and it held the last small trembling roses of summer, yellow and almost faded, deliciously fragrant. When the butler had silently collected up all the debris, Courilof was ashamed; he gestured for him to go away. Then he shrugged his shoulders, looked at me and said: 'We can be so childish!'

He sat motionless for a long time, his eyes lowered.

In the afternoon, he would go and lie down, spending long hours on his settee, reading. He called for stacks of books, armfuls of them, French novels whose pages he meticulously cut to pass the time. He would slip the blade between the pages, smooth them out, then cut them apart with little slicing movements. Lost in thought, he never made a sound.

I often saw him staring into space with his wide, sad eyes, holding a large book open in front of him. Then he would look at the last page, sigh and throw the book down.

'I'm bored,' he said over and over again, 'I'm so bored!'

He'd start pacing back and forth in his bedroom, a room filled with many icons. When his wife came in, his face would light up, but almost immediately, he'd look away and start wandering aimlessly from room to room again.

The few people who called to see him were sent away. He was reading the *Life of the Saints*, I recall, and pretended it was some consolation to him. But since he was so attached to worldly possessions, to physical pleasures, he also dismissed religious books with a sigh.

'God will forgive me . . . We are all just poor sinners.' He had pretensions of being European, so found his involuntary sighs more disconcerting than anyone else did.

There was only one thing he never tired of, one thing that he really loved. He gestured for me to sit down opposite him: he had some tea and lamps brought in. It already felt like autumn; a misty fog fell on to the Iles at dusk, dense and full of shadows. Then the Killer Whale would tell me about his past. For hours at a time, he would talk about himself: his services to the monarchy, his family, his childhood, his opinions about the role of a great politician. But on the rare occasions he deigned to talk about men he'd known, he surprised me. He found a bitterly funny way of describing them. He talked about their petty intrigues, the misappropriation of public funds, their thefts and betrayals, so commonplace in the city and at court, a bizarre crowd who amused me.

I think it's because of Courilof that I was later able to

give some good advice to the rulers of the time to help them manage things. This was when the glorious days of the Revolution were over and we had to deal with Europe and the growing demands of the people. He taught me more than he ever knew, my old enemy; and it was just the opposite of what he thought he was teaching me . . .

Often I wasn't even listening to what he said, just to his tone of voice, tinged with bitterness and venom; I watched his ghostly pale, haughty face, already marked by death and devoured by envy and ambition. A small mahogany table with two old-fashioned lamps and painted metal shades sat between us. Their flames burned peacefully in the dark. You could hear the policemen, ever present like me, even though they no longer had a minister to protect; they made their rounds beneath the windows, whispering softly as they passed each other in the night.

'Men . . . men,' repeated Courilof. 'Ministers, princes, what puppets they all are! True power lies in the hands of madmen or children, who don't even know they have it. The rest of humanity is chasing after shadows!'

That was exactly how he spoke: he was a man who lacked simplicity, but also managed to speak the truth.

Then came another silent dinner. Afterwards, Marguerite Eduardovna played the piano as we paced back and forth through the great reception room: the sparkling wooden floors reflected the lights from the chandeliers, all lit up for his solitary stroll. Sometimes, he would stop and shout in frustration: 'Tomorrow I'm leaving!'

And the next day would be exactly the same.

24

Meanwhile, the troubles in the capital continued. From the universities, the problems spread to the factories where, in certain provinces, bloody battles broke out once more. Dahl didn't know how to deal with either the schools or the universities.

One evening, Courilof seemed more animated than usual. As he was saying good night to me, he added: 'Don't go to St Petersburg tomorrow: the students at the Imperial Secondary Schools intend to present a petition to the Emperor, who is currently at the Winter Palace, in support of the striking workers in the Poutilov factories.'

'What's going to happen?' I asked.

He laughed curtly. 'No one knows anything yet, and His Excellency' – he stressed the words sarcastically, as always when he mentioned his successor – 'His Excellency knows even less than anyone. It will end quite simply. The commander at the palace will be caught off guard and will call in the troops. When that happens, power automatically passes to the colonel, and since there will be no lack of protestors to insult the army, the soldiers will be forced to open fire. That's what will happen,' he said, forcing a little laugh. 'That's where it will all end – with a minister like Baron Dahl who treats the children he's responsible for as if they were dogs!'

I said nothing.

'It could prove very damaging to him,' Courilof murmured pensively.

I asked why, and Courilof started laughing again and patted me on the shoulder; his large hand was unusually strong.

'So you're interested in these events, are you? You don't understand? You really don't understand?' he repeated. (He seemed enormously amused.) 'Do you think the Emperor will be pleased to see dead bodies underneath his windows? Such things are perfectly acceptable as long as they happen far from view . . .' (he suddenly frowned, no doubt recalling some inconvenient facts), 'but not right in front of you, at your home. Do you know what Emperor Alexander I is supposed to have said? "Princes sometimes like crime, but they rarely like criminals." That's a good one, don't you think? And then of course there's the press; even though they are conveniently censored here, thank God, they still have some influence.'

He went over to his wife and took her arm. 'You see, my darling, personally, I am very happy not to be taking such risks, no longer having these problems,' he said, in French, forcing his voice to sound light-hearted and indifferent. 'Yes indeed, this has made me feel better! I admit I foolishly allowed myself to fall into a kind of depression. Next week we'll leave for Vevey, my darling. We shall cultivate our garden. Do you remember the seagulls by the lake? Unless of course . . .'

And he drifted off, dreamily. 'Those poor children!' he spat, thoughtful and grave. 'Now there are truly innocent souls for whom *they* must answer before God.'

He stood silent for a long time, sighed, then took Marguerite Eduardovna's hand. 'Let's go upstairs, my dear.'

Just then, the bell rang downstairs. He jumped; it was nearly midnight. A servant entered, saying there was a small group of men who didn't wish to give their names, asking to see him at once. His wife begged him not to let them in.

'They're anarchists, revolutionaries,' she kept saying, anxiously.

'Let me go with you,' I said to Courilof. 'With the two of us and the servants within earshot, we'll be safe.'

He agreed, doubtlessly to appease his wife: I knew how naturally calm and courageous he was. Still, he suspected something wasn't right and it made him curious. Whatever the reason, he agreed. The visitors were taken downstairs to the empty office. They apologised for having come so late at night, without having requested an audience. It was a delegation of teachers from the Imperial Secondary Schools; they were pale and shaking as they huddled by the door, afraid to come in, petrified by the heavy, fixed stare of the Killer Whale. As for my Courilof, he proudly stood up straight, as tall as a peacock. He let his hand drop on to the desk in his usual way; it was a large, powerful hand. It was white and freckled, adorned with a large gemstone ring, a garnet that caught the light and gleamed blood-red.

The teachers were old and frightened. They said they'd

come to try to prevent something terrible from happening. The Minister of Education had refused to see them. A scornful little smile hovered over Courilof's lips . . . They had come to beg His Excellency to please warn Dahl, whom they believed was indebted to Courilof as his former colleague, his friend. (They had no idea that Dahl had stolen the post from Courilof; in the city, the official story was that Courilof had to retire for health reasons; the secrets of the gods were carefully guarded. The important people at the court knew every detail of what had happened, naturally, but the secondary school teachers were hardly important people there.) Just as Courilof had said, a delegation of young people had decided to present a request to the Emperor, asking him to pardon the strikers who'd been deported. The teachers feared the children would be mistaken for strikers and shot. (Two years later, this is exactly what would happen to the workers led by G . . . in front of the Winter Palace.)

The longer he listened to them, the paler and more silent Courilof became. This man's silences had extraordinary power; he seemed frozen into a block of ice.

'What do you want me to do, gentlemen?' he finally said.

'Warn Baron Dahl. He'll listen to you. Or at least ask him to receive us. You will be preventing something awful, much loss of life.'

They didn't realise that my Courilof was thinking of only one thing: how to seize the opportunity, offered to him by fate, to throw his successor into an impossible situation. He could first reclaim his job, then, later on when the moment was right, he would be hailed as the defender and saviour of the monarchy. I felt I could read his mind. I don't know why, but I imagined he was quoting *deus ex machina* to himself, in Latin, as he liked to do.

'I cannot do it, gentlemen: what you are asking of me is quite improper. I have retired from public life, not because of my health, as you thought, but because the Emperor wished it. Go and see Baron Dahl yourself. Insist.'

'But he refused to see us!'

'Well then, gentlemen, what can I do? . . . I am powerless.'

They begged him. One of them was a pale old man in a black coat. Suddenly he leaned forward and (I can still picture it) grabbed Courilof's hand and kissed it.

'My son is one of the leaders, Your Excellency; please save my son!'

'You shouldn't have allowed him to get mixed up in this,' said Courilof, his voice icy and sharp. 'Go home and lock your son in.'

The old man gestured in despair. 'So you refuse?'

'Gentlemen, I cannot intervene, I repeat, it's got nothing to do with me.'

Quietly they conferred with one another; then they began to all talk at once, imploring this motionless man.

'Their blood will be on your hands,' one of them said, his voice shaking.

'It won't be the first time,' said Courilof, smiling slightly. 'Nor will it be the first time I've been held responsible for blood I haven't spilled.'

They left.

The next day, before they reached the gates of the Winter Palace, the thirty young people were stopped by the army. As the army tried to disperse them, someone grabbed the reins of one of the horses. The Cossack felt his horse rear and thought he was being attacked; he fired. The youngsters responded by throwing stones; the crowd angrily took sides and a shower of stones fell against the bronze gates and the Imperial Eagles that decorated them. The colonel ordered his men to open fire. Fifteen people were killed: students and passers-by (amongst the first shot was the son of the elderly gentleman who had come to beg Courilof's help), and all right under the Emperor's windows. The scandal caused by the death of these fifteen victims would rid Courilof of Dahl and return him to his post as Minister of Education.

25

Naturally, it didn't happen immediately; for a long time, even I knew nothing about it.

The following week, Courilof and his family left for the Caucasus, and I went with them.

Their house was not far from Kislovodsk, at the very edge of the city. From its large, circular wooden balcony, you could see the first foothills of the mountains. It was extremely beautiful, though arid and bare, with the occasional dark cypress tree surrounded by stones and water. In the garden, there were wild rose-bushes in bloom; they had twisted branches, spiky thorns, and flowers whose perfume filled the evening air. Just like here in France, they grew in clusters, beneath the windows.

The air was too chilly for me; I couldn't stop coughing.

One day, Dahl arrived. He seemed perfectly calm. He told us he'd come to relax in the spa at Kislovodsk, take the waters of Kislovodsk, and that the moment he'd arrived, he'd immediately come to see 'his dear friend'. During the meal, he openly told all of us how he had been unfairly blamed for the events in August.

'Once again, "they" found their scapegoat,' he said, smiling. 'And this time, it was yours truly.'

(The expressions 'they', 'you know who', 'those people', all meant the imperial family and the grand dukes. My Courilof also often used these terms as well.)

'It's a sad story,' Dahl added, shrugging his shoulders with indifference. Most likely it was feigned, for he too had the pleasure of gathering up the dead bodies at nightfall. I had noticed they were all stony faced when it happened behind their backs; but when they actually saw the massacred children with their own eyes, touched them with their own hands, that was different. 'If only I could have known what they were plotting . . . I heard the entire city knew what was going on, but *I*, well, I was the last to know. That's always the way it is. So there you have it! The Emperor considerately asked me to tender my resignation. His Majesty, in his great kindness, deigned to promise me a post in the senate and also asked my advice, even in my disgrace, about who to eventually name as my successor. Moreover, to top off his goodness, he kindly appointed my son secretary to the embassy in Copenhagen. It's a city that doesn't maintain the same importance as in our day, Valerian Alexandrovitch, but the imperial couple go there often enough to make the post desirable. We're lucky to end up anywhere the sun spreads its rays, if you'll allow me the metaphor.'

He said no more, and changed the subject.

After lunch, the two former ministers went into Courilof's office, where they remained for a long time.

Froelich nudged me to point out Irène Valerianovna's worried expression.

'I think that the old fox has come to negotiate his son's marriage to Mademoiselle Ina,' he whispered.

That evening, Dahl stayed for dinner; he was very happy and several times before leaving, he kissed the young girl's hand. This was very unlike him and clearly gave away his intentions. After he'd gone, Courilof wanted to see Irène Valerianovna, but she'd gone up to her room. It was the next morning, in front of me – for they thought I knew no Russian – that Courilof spoke to his daughter.

He complained of having been in pain all night long; when his daughter came in to say good morning the next day, he asked her to stay.

'Ina,' he said solemnly. 'Baron Dahl has done me the honour of asking for your hand in marriage for his son. We had discussed this last year . . .'

She cut in. 'I know,' she said quietly, 'but I don't love him.'

'There are serious considerations at stake, my child,' said Courilof in his haughtiest tone.

'I know Dahl doesn't just want my dowry for his son, and that you . . .'

He blushed suddenly and banged his fist against the table in anger. 'That does not concern you. You will be married, rich and free. What else do you want?'

'That's it, isn't it?' she asked, ignoring what he'd said. 'You want an alliance with the baron, don't you? He's promised to get you back your miserable post as minister if I agree, hasn't he? That's it, isn't it?'

'Yes,' said Courilof. 'You understand, you're not stupid.

But why do you think I want the post?' he continued, and I could have sworn he was being sincere. 'It's my cross to bear and will send me to an early grave, for I'm not well, not at all well, my child, but I must serve my Emperor, my country and those unfortunate children being led to their downfall by the revolutionaries. I must serve them with all my strength and until I breathe my last. I must watch over them, punish them if necessary, but as a father would do, not as an enemy. Certainly not like Dahl, whose guilty negligence got them killed. And it is quite true that the baron promised to help me if you agree to this marriage. The Emperor holds him in great esteem; it is only public opinion following this unfortunate event that has forced him to distance himself from Dahl. Of course, Dahl has hardly behaved brilliantly,' he continued, sounding disgusted, 'but it is up to God to judge him . . . As far as I'm concerned, my conscience is clear. Moreover, Dahl comes from an honourable family that was often allied with ours in the past. It is natural to wish to increase one's worldly possessions by marrying wealth . . . and, my poor girl, as for love . . .'

He stopped: he'd been speaking French as he usually did when the conversation turned to higher or sensitive subjects. He frowned and turned towards me. 'Please leave us, my dear Monsieur Legrand; I do apologise.'

I went out.

That same evening, Courilof took his daughter's arm, and they strolled along an isolated little path where they could sit together. When they returned, he seemed happy; his face had taken on its normal solemn expression. His daughter, very pale, smiled sadly, ironically.

That night, I went out on the balcony. Irène Valerianovna was sitting very still, her head in her hands. The moon was very bright, and I could clearly see the young girl's white nightdress and her bare arms holding the hand-rail. She was crying. I understood she had given her consent and that everything was going to change, which is exactly what happened.

Shortly afterwards, the engagement was made official. And finally one morning, his hands trembling, Courilof opened a package that I could see contained a small photograph of the Empress and two of her children, supreme proof of their reconciliation. Courilof hung the picture in a gold frame above his desk, just below the icon.

All that remained was to wait for a telegram from the Emperor informing Courilof that he was to be reinstated to the post of minister, assuming his improved health would henceforth allow him to resume his public duties. All of us were waiting for this telegram, in fact, and all with different emotions. It arrived in the middle of September. Courilof gathered everyone around and read it out loud to the whole family, made a large sign of the cross, and said, tears in his eyes:

'Once again the great burden of power falls upon my shoulders, but God will help me bear it.'

26

I felt strange: I was devastated, but at the same time, understood the intensely bitter joke destiny had played on us.

It was nearly time to go back; every day Courilof seemed happier and in better health. The weather was beautiful, golden. I had grown accustomed to the mountain air; at times, I felt a kind of drowsiness and calm; while at other moments, I was so tired of the world that I felt like smashing my head against the rocks. Those beautiful red rocks; I remember them: they were like the rocks here ...

One evening I made my decision. I announced I was urgently needed back in Switzerland. I would leave the next day; I said I needed to speak to the minister.

After dinner (it was nearly eight o'clock and the sun was setting) Courilof was in the habit of going for a walk before tea was served later in the evening. He took the path in front of the terrace and, from there, walked up a narrow road lined with rocks. I went with him.

I remember the sound the stones made under our feet; they were round and shiny and reddish beneath the setting sun. But the sky was tinted violet, and under its mournful, dazzling light, Courilof's face took on a strange expression.

There were waterfalls above; great torrents crashed down and echoed off the rocks angrily. We walked past them, climbed higher still, and it was there that I told him I had considered the matter seriously and was leaving. I said I felt it was my duty as a doctor to tell him he was undoubtedly more ill than he thought. I believed he should take better care of himself, give up any unnecessary activities; if he did, he would live longer.

He listened to me, his face impassive, without moving a muscle. When I had finished, he stared at me calmly. I can still picture that look.

'But my dear Monsieur Legrand, I am quite aware of my condition. My father died of liver cancer, you know.' He fell silent, sighing. 'No good Christian fears death so long as he has fulfilled his duty here on earth,' he said (and little by little, his sincere voice turned solemn and pompous again). 'I intend to accomplish much in my few remaining years before sleeping in eternal peace.'

I asked if I had understood him correctly, that he refused to give up his public duties, knowing what he now knew. I always suspected, I added, that he was aware of his condition, despite what that idiot Langenberg said; but did he realise that liver cancer progresses quickly, and that he had only months to live, a year at the most?

'Of course,' he replied, shrugging his shoulders. 'I willingly put myself in God's hands.'

'I think that when a man is facing death, it is better to give up any work that could be harmful, in order to achieve peace of mind,' I said.

He winced. 'Harmful! Good Lord! My work is my only consolation! I am the holy guardian of the traditions of the Empire! I shall be able to say, just as Augustus did as he was dying: *Plaudicite amici, bene agi actum vitae*! Applaud friends, I have acted well in life!'

He could have gone on in the same vein for a long time. He had no regrets . . . I cut in. I tried to speak as simply and sarcastically as possible.

'Valerian Alexandrovitch, don't you think it's terrible? You know very well that what you did caused the deaths of innocent people, and will cause many more. I am not a politician, but I do wonder if that ever keeps you awake at night?'

He sat silently. The sun had set, so I could no longer see his face. Still, since I was very close to him, I saw how he tilted his head towards his shoulder. He looked like a dark block of stone.

'Every action, every battle, brings death. If we are on this earth, it is to act and destroy. But when one is acting for a higher cause . . .' He stopped and then said, 'It isn't easy to live a good life.' His voice had changed; it was softer and tinged with sadness. I think it was his frankness, these flashes of sincerity that made him so charming and yet so frustrating.

He stood up, calling over his shoulder, 'Shall we go back?'

We retraced our steps in silence. It was very dark now, and we had to be careful of the stones and low brambles that got caught on our clothes. In front of the house, he shook my hand. 'Good-bye, Monsieur Legrand. Have a good trip; we'll see each other again one day, I hope.'

I said that anything was possible, and we parted.

Very early the following morning, I was awakened by the sound of footsteps and muffled voices in the garden. I leaned forward to look out of the window and through the wooden slats, I saw my Courilof with a policeman; he was easily recognisable in spite of his disguise. I remembered seeing this policeman on several occasions when he accompanied the minister to give his reports to the Emperor. I realised that Courilof was having me followed. As usual, he wasn't very clever about it; but it was the one and only moment during all the time I spent with him that I suddenly understood what it truly meant to hate. Seeing this powerful man, so confident, calmly standing in his garden, knowing that all he had to do was say the word and I would be tracked down, locked up and hung like an animal, made me understand how easy it can be to kill in cold blood. At that very moment, I could have happily held a gun to his head and pulled the trigger.

In the meantime, I had to get away, which I did. I openly took the train to St Petersburg, followed by the policeman; in the middle of the night, got off at one of the little mountain stations. From there, I made it to the Persian border. I remained in Persia for a few days; I exchanged my Swiss passport for the identity papers of a carpet salesman, given to me by some members of a revolutionary group in Tehran. Towards the end of September, I went back to Russia.

I arrived in St Petersburg and went straight to Fanny's place; she settled me into her room and then went out. I was tired, utterly exhausted. I threw myself down on the bed and immediately fell asleep.

I remember a dream I had, which is rare for me. My dream was very beautiful, very innocent; it seemed to rise up from the depths of an idyllic childhood, for I was young, handsome, and bursting with energy in a way I'd never really been. I stood in a meadow full of flowers bathed in sunlight; the most bizarre thing was that the children standing around me were Courilof, Prince Nelrode, Dahl, Schwann and the stranger from Vevey. In the end, it turned into a painful, indescribably grotesque nightmare: their faces changed, becoming old and tired, yet they continued running and playing as before.

I woke up and saw Fanny come into the room, followed by a comrade I knew. But he didn't look as wonderfully calm as the first time we'd met: he seemed worried and annoyed. He warned me that the police had been alerted, they were already looking for me, and I was to take every precaution. I let him talk. I was so utterly frustrated by then that I felt I wanted to be done with him, as well as Courilof.

He looked at me oddly, and I'm convinced he had me followed from that day on, right up until the assassination. His men were better at it than Courilof's spies, but the minute I stepped out the door, I could sense them behind me.

October had arrived. It got dark early and it was relatively easy to slip away at a street corner. It hadn't started snowing yet, but the air had that icy heaviness peculiar to autumn in Russia; the lamps in the houses were lit from early morning. A misty, snowy fog rose up and sat low on the ground; the earth was frozen, hollow. A sad time . . . I spent hours on end stretched out on the bed, in the room Fanny had given up for me. I was coughing up blood; I had the smell and taste of blood in my mouth and on my skin.

I didn't see Fanny any more; it had been agreed that she would come to see me the night before the assassination to give the final order, since she was the one responsible for preparing the bombs and giving them to me. The comrade came to see me again, telling me the exact time to go through with it: eleven forty-five. There was no question of going inside the theatre itself, as it was by invitation only, so we'd have to wait at the entrance.

'If you hadn't been found out,' he said bitterly, 'it would have been so simple! Courilof would have got you a seat in the theatre and during the interval you could have gone into his box and shot him! All those months we tailed him, for what! Now, with these bloody bombs, you risk killing twenty innocent people for one Courilof.'

'I don't give a damn,' I replied.

Nothing had ever seemed as ridiculous to me as their false precautions. When he asked me: 'What? If Courilof were in a carriage with his wife and children, you'd throw the bomb?' I said yes, and I thought I actually could have done it. What difference would it make? But I could see he didn't believe me.

'Well, comrade,' he finally said, 'that won't happen. He'll be alone with his servants.'

They, apparently, didn't count.

'Well, good-bye then!' he said.

He left.

It happened the next evening. Fanny came with me. We were carrying bombs covered in shawls and wrapped in parcel paper. We didn't speak. We went and sat down in a brightly lit little square opposite the Marie Theatre. A long line of policemen and carriages waited in the street.

The square was empty. The sky was low and dark; a fine, light snow fluttered through the air, turning to rain as soon as it touched the ground. Tiny needles of icy rain that stung your face.

Fanny pointed to the parked carriages. 'The court, the diplomatic corps, the German Embassy delegation, the ministers,' she whispered with a kind of exultation.

The night was deadly long, terrible. Around eleven o'clock, the wind changed and a thick snow began to fall. We moved to another spot; we were frozen. Twice we walked around the little square.

Suddenly we found ourselves face to face with someone who'd emerged from the shadows to look at us. Fanny pressed herself against me and I kissed her. Thinking we were lovers, the policeman was reassured and disappeared. I held Fanny in my arms; she looked up at me, and I remember that, for the first time, I saw a tear in those cruel eyes.

I let go of her. We continued to walk in silence. I was coughing. Blood kept rushing into my mouth. I spat it out, then coughed again; blood trickled on to my hands. I wanted to lay down right there in the snow and die.

The carriages began to move forward. You could hear the sound of doors opening and banging shut inside the theatre, and the shrill whistles of the policemen.

I crossed the street. I was holding a bomb in my hand as if it were a flower. It was grotesque. I don't understand how no one noticed and arrested me. Fanny followed behind. We stopped close to the entrance, beneath the columns heavy with snow, between the rows of people.

The doors opened. Everyone came out. The Emperor, the imperial family, William II and his entourage had already left. I saw women in furs walk by, jewellery gleaming beneath their delicate mantillas dotted with snowflakes. There were generals whose spurs clattered against the frozen ground, and others as well, people I didn't know, the doddery old fools of the diplomatic corps, and still others . . . Courilof. He turned towards me; his face was old and pale; or was it just the light from the street-lamps that made his features seem so furrowed? He looked weary and defeated, with big dark circles under his eyes. I turned towards Fanny.

'I can't kill him,' I said.

I felt her grab the bomb from me. She took two steps forward and threw it.

I remember a jumble of faces, hands, eyes, that swam around in front of me, then disappeared in explosion with the noise and light of hell itself. We weren't hurt, but our faces were cut, our clothes burnt, our hands covered in blood. I took Fanny's hand and we ran through the dark streets, ran like hunted animals. People were bumping into us, rushing in all directions. Several of them had ripped clothes and bloody hands, like us. An injured horse whinnied so horribly from pain that shivers ran down my spine. When we finally stopped, we were in the middle of a square, surrounded by an angry crowd. I knew we were finished. I felt relieved. It was there we were arrested.

Afterwards, Fanny and I found ourselves in a room next to the one where the dead bodies were piled up. We had guards, but amidst the confusion and horror, it hadn't occurred to them to separate us.

Fanny suddenly burst into tears. I felt sorry for her. I'd already said that I was the one who'd thrown the bomb, as that was only fair: if she hadn't grabbed it from my hands, I would have ended up throwing it. That . . . that was the easy part . . . And anyway, as I've already said, I was coughing up so much blood that I felt there was none left in my lungs; I was certain that if they just let me close my eyes and sit still, I would die; and I painfully, eagerly longed for that moment.

I went over to Fanny, put a cigarette in her hand and whispered:

'You have nothing to worry about.'

She shook her head. 'It's not that, it's not that . . . Dead! He's dead! Dead!'

'Who's dead?' I asked, confused.

'Courilof! He's dead! Dead! And I'm the one who killed him!'

Nevertheless, her instinct for survival remained strong within her.

When the policeman came closer, attracted by her cries, he heard her say again: 'He's dead! And we're the ones who killed him!'

And so she was condemned to life in prison and I to be hanged.

But you should never count on death any more than you count on life. I'm still here . . . The devil alone knows why. Later on, Fanny escaped and took part in a second assassination. She was the one who killed P . . . in 1907 or 1908. She was caught, and this time, she hung herself in her cell. As for me . . . Well, I've told my story. Life is absurd. Fortunately for me, at least, the show will soon be over.

Translator's Afterword

When Irène Némirovsky's *Suite Française* was first published, many critics were astonished by the author's remarkable ability to 'write history' as events unfolded – without the benefit of hindsight. In *The Courilof Affair*, however, first published in French by Grasset in 1933, she bases her novel on an historical event. In 1901, a student named Karpovitch assassinated the former Russian Minister of Education, Nikolaï Bogoliepov. Némirovsky's novel deals with the issue of terrorism and the moral questions it raises.

It is interesting to compare *The Courilof Affair* to two French plays on exactly the same theme, one by Jean-Paul Sartre and the other by Albert Camus. More than fifteen years after Némirovsky's novel was published, Sartre's *Les Mains Sales* (*Dirty Hands*, 1948) and Camus' *Les Justes* (*The Just Assassins*, first performed in 1949) explore the same problem.

Sartre's examination of the theme is clearly from an Existentialist viewpoint, highlighting his basic philosophical concepts of freedom, choice and acting in *bonne foi* or *mauvaise foi* (good or bad faith). His protagonist, Hugo, is charged with assassinating Hoederer, the leader of the 'Party' who is regarded as a traitor by a small faction of the same group. He infiltrates Hoederer's home by posing as a secretary, but, like Némirovsky's Léon M, as Hugo gets to know Hoederer, his resolve weakens. Unlike Léon M, however, Hugo gradually becomes convinced of the correctness of Hoederer's position. Hugo's emotional, impulsive 'act' of assassination is finally determined by petty jealousy, a classic Sartrean example of 'bad faith', and results in disastrous personal consequences for Hugo. At the end of the play, Hugo is disillusioned with both the Party and life itself.

Like *The Courilof Affair*, Camus' play *Les Justes* is based on an historical event, the assassination of the Grand Duke Sergei Romanov by a Russian Socialist-Revolutionary in 1905. In Camus' version, the idealist poet, Kaliayev (he uses the actual historical name for his protagonist), and Stepan, a sceptical, experienced assassin, symbolise opposing philosophical perspectives. Kaliayev struggles to accept Stepan's belief that 'the ends justify the means' and is finally given the opportunity of proving himself to the terrorist group by being allowed to throw the bomb. But as the Imperial carriage approaches, Kaliayev sees that there are two children with the Grand Duke, and scruples prevent him from taking their innocent lives. After much debate and soul-searching, Kaliayev finally carries out the assassination when the Grand Duke is alone, and is arrested. He tells his interrogator, Skouratov: *'J'ai lancé la bombe sur votre tyrannie, non sur un homme'* ('I threw the bomb at your tyranny, not at a man'), to which Skouratov replies: *'Mais c'est l'homme qui l'a reçue'* ('But it was the man who was killed'). Camus then writes a most innovative scene between the Grand Duchesse and Kaliayev, in which the widow of the man he has killed tries to help him repent and find forgiveness.

Camus had previously dealt with this very question in his outstanding *Lettres à un ami allemand* (*Letters to a German Friend*), in which he clearly states that there are some means that simply cannot be justified. He would explore similar themes in *L'Homme révolté* (*The Rebel*), 1951, a work that basically demonstrates the futility of all revolutions, showing how the positive urge to create a more just, utopian society ultimately deteriorates into a cycle of tyranny and counter-revolution. Némirovsky's family experienced this first-hand when they were forced to flee Russia during the 1917 Revolution.

Camus comes to the conclusion that most political 'causes', even ones that began with the best intentions, soon deteriorate into a quest for personal power, status and wealth.

Had Sartre and Camus read Némirovsky's *The Courilof Affair* when it was first published in 1933? Impossible to say. Camus was 20 years old and living in Algeria at the time, working on a degree in Philosophy. Sartre was 28 and studying phenomenology with Husserl in Berlin. In Olivier Philipponnat and Patrick Lienhardt's excellent new biography of Irène Némirovsky, they state that in 1938, the literary critic Maxence wrote a review in which he said that he preferred Némirovsky's *La Proie* to Sartre's *La Nausée*, so it is probable that Sartre knew her work.

It would be fascinating to know whether Sartre and Camus had read *The Courilof Affair*, but it is not vital. Clearly, the theme of terrorism and when, if ever, it is justified, was foremost in their minds after their experience of living under Nazi Occupation during World War II.

Unfortunately, in current times, we too are familiar with the moral and philosophical problem of terrorism. After the attacks in Paris on 3 December 1996, in America on 11 September 2001, in Madrid on 11 March 2004, in London on 7 July 2005, and countless others, our world has changed. Terrorism is no longer a theoretical question: we face it every time we travel, walk down a crowded city street or read a newspaper.

Literature will always reflect life. The essential question today is whether we can truly learn the lessons that literature attempts to teach.

Sandra Smith, Fellow
Robinson College,
Cambridge, May 2008